Where the Fireflies Dance

Kate Grasso

Copyright © 2023 by Kate Grasso

All rights reserved.

No portion of this book may be reproduced in any form without written permission from the publisher or author, except as permitted by U.S. copyright law.

Although every precaution has been taken to verify the accuracy of the information contained herein, no responsibility is assumed for any errors or omissions, and no liability is assumed for damages that may result from the use of this information.

This book is a work of fiction. Any references to historical events, real people, or real places are used fictitiously. Other names, characters, places, and events are products of the author's imagination, and any resemblance to actual events, places, or persons, living or dead, is entirely coincidental.

Kate Grasso and Disney Cicerone are not associated with The Walt Disney Company. The views expressed in this book are those of the author alone and do not reflect those of The Walt Disney Company.

Book cover by Kate Grasso.

Contents

		v
1.	Chapter 1	1
2.	Chapter 2	6
3.	Chapter 3	12
4.	Chapter 4	21
5.	Chapter 5	31
6.	Chapter 6	42
7.	Chapter 7	54
8.	Chapter 8	65
9.	Chapter 9	72
10.	Chapter 10	82
11.	Chapter 11	92
12.	Chapter 12	100
13.	Chapter 13	109
14.	Chapter 14	120
15.	Chapter 15	125
16.	Chapter 16	132
17.	Epilogue	143
	A Note from the Author	150
	About the Author	152

Also By Kate Grasso 153

Bibliography 155

"Disneyland liberates men to their better selves."

Ray Bradbury, 1958

Chapter 1

Leah

I bit into my churro and savored the moment as the warmed cinnamon and sugar hit my tongue. This was the moment I looked forward to each day, the time I reserved for myself to simply *be* at Disneyland. I turned off my phone's screen, shelved each anxious thought, and tucked my skirt under me, crossing my ankles in a ladylike fashion as I settled on the shady concrete bench.

The band jubilantly played an instrumental cover of *Frozen*'s "Into the Unknown" in the space in front of the castle and my mind automatically filled in the blanks of the missing lyrics to the all-too-familiar song.

So much of my life now was about the unknown, and it was terrifying and freeing all at the same time.

I wasn't used to being able to think about the future.

Max made sure of that.

I shook my head as if I could erase those thoughts as easily.

No. I reminded myself. *Not here. Never here.*

You are safe here.

I briskly brushed the sugary crumbs off my vintage circle skirt and huffed out a breath, frustrated at how easily my mind traveled back to him.

I abruptly pushed to stand, bobbing and weaving my way around throngs of tourists taking photos on my way to the trash can. I always appreciated Walt Disney's insight of placing trash cans thirty feet from any given location to try to encourage a tidy park. After disposing of my churro trash, I moved toward my favorite ride, anxious to clear the thoughts racing around like Chip & Dale in my head.

It was exhausting to always wonder if I was safe. If I needed to glance over my shoulder just one more time, just in case. If I would ever shake the gnawing sense of dread that only seemed to ease when I ran through my mental checklist to ensure I had not left anything to chance.

I swayed back and forth to the cheery music of Main Street, letting my skirt swish around me as I peeked up at the castle for one last moment of inspiration. The Violet-Le-Duc spire on the top was my favorite of the golden touches, a part of the castle that did not belong in any way, shape, or form to the style of architecture the rest of Sleeping Beauty Castle inhabited. It was a beautiful homage to the spire that used to grace Notre Dame Cathedral in Paris, and Walt approved its expense while his brother Roy was out of town. It was pure indulgence. Walt wanted it because he wanted it. Not because it made sense, was integral to the design, or was structurally important. It was simply beauty for beauty's sake, and it made my heart ache at the sight. I needed to be reminded that such a sentiment was possible because my world had become an ugly place, indeed.

Walking across the drawbridge that had only been raised twice in Disneyland's history, I hummed along to the ever-present song in the castle tunnel, wanting to believe with all my being that anything my heart desired could come true. I'd been wishing on stars my whole life, and I wasn't about to stop now. Like a bolt out of the blue, the carousel appeared before me, sparkling in the sunlight like my mother's rhinestone Mickey necklace that rested just above my heart, always. The carousel drew me in, the seductress that she was, all gold accents and gleaming white ponies just begging for riders. I was forever hooked.

Waltzing my way forward, I promised myself that I could go on just this one ride on my own before pulling my phone back out and going live on social media again. I knew that time was precious and every minute of streaming could mean more followers and more income to keep me in this place of safety, but I just needed … Walt. A moment for a conversation with someone who understood how hard it was to fall on your face and have to get back up again. Someone who knew what it meant to desperately struggle after losing everything and yet not let go of your dreams.

As I made my way around to the entrance of the carousel line, I saw a hand waving from the exit of Mr. Toad before I heard my friend Colette's call over the cacophony of Fantasyland.

"Leah!"

I smiled as she hustled towards me, deftly dodging strollers and scooters in what I would swear was a choreographed dance if I didn't know better.

Colette, more commonly known as CreativelyColette, was a pro. She had been in the parks creating content for over eight years but she never let her rise to social media fame change her. She was a 100% real-life princess and villain all rolled into one, with a dash of Cheshire Cat tossed into the mix just to keep things interesting. Colette was self-confident, stubborn, utterly beguiling, and always true to who she was.

How did she do it?

I marveled at her capacity to keep her heart on her sleeve and her laughter loud in all circumstances, wishing that I could encompass even a tiny drop of the magic she held just by existing.

"Hey, Colette," I offered as she drew near, her beloved camera in hand. "What are you up to?"

"Oh, just trying to see if I can catch a ride on that original 1955 Mr. Toad car they installed. You know, the one with the lights on it. I've been through the queue three times and I still can't seem to catch it. I asked the Cast Members if I could wait for it but because it's so popular, they said, 'Sorry, no.'"

"Oh, man. Sorry to hear that Col. Maybe wait for a bit and give it another try?"

"Oh, I'm not giving up. You know me. I'll ride all day if I have to, I need to get this shot."

I laughed. She wasn't kidding. *Stubborn* could easily be Colette's middle name, and she'd proven it on more occasions than I could count. Sometimes she tried to convince me to do crazy things though, like break the record for the most consecutive rides on Casey Jr. Train, but while I always supported such feats of bladder control, I wasn't looking for fame.

I was looking for peace.

I sighed. I envied Colette's life, her vivacity and charm that I couldn't match if I tried. The world literally was her oyster—and not the little ones with the unfortunate fate from *Alice in Wonderland*.

"Well good luck, my dear. If anyone can do it, you can," I said with an encouraging smile.

Colette brushed her red hair back over her shoulder and tossed a glance back at Mr. Toad's stone smile from his perch over the entrance door before turning her attention back to me. "Thanks, Leah. What's up with you? I saw you were taking a break from your live stream today, everything ok?"

I felt my smile start to melt but caught myself before it fell away entirely, holding a strained grin that I hoped looked real to Colette. She didn't know about Max, and I had to keep it that way. It was safer for her.

Ordinarily, I was able to hide my emotions better, but on top of the usual mess that was my life, it was my dad's birthday. Or would have been, if he was still around.

Sometimes I could still hear him call me his Princess Leah. Could feel his arms around me as he told me that I was brave, beautiful, and strong.

It hurt to know I'd never hear him say any of it ever again.

But Colette didn't need to know this any more than she needed to know my true secrets, so I just shrugged instead, giving her a simple answer that didn't invite more questions.

"Yeah, I was just getting my churro fix. You know me. Sugar addict and all that," I said, grimacing at the lameness of my response, positive that she could see right through it.

Colette raised an eyebrow just like Walt used to do when he wasn't satisfied with something. Clearly, she wasn't convinced, but she knew me well enough to know that I don't offer personal details about my life, and she was kind enough not to push me. "Well, let me know if you need anything. I'm headed back to Toad Hall. Maybe this time I won't end up in hell."

She smiled and winked before dancing her way back to the queue, her camera already rolling and capturing the footage she needed to make her living.

I watched her go and sighed. I wondered if there would ever be a time when I could trust someone, just let them in a little. Not all the way … no, never that. But maybe a little wouldn't hurt.

I pondered the idea throughout the monotony of the carousel queue, turning it around in my brain like a Rubik's cube, trying to make my hope and reality line up in a way that made sense.

But as I climbed onto Walt's favorite horse Jingles, giving my customary pat to the umbrella on the back in deference to Mary Poppins, I threw my imaginary Rubik's cube in frustration. There was no solving this puzzle.

And as the carousel turned around again and again, I saw a reflection of my own life in each rotation, going around and around and never moving forward.

I leaned my forehead against the cool metal of the pole and squeezed my eyes tight to hold back the hot tears that threatened to make themselves known. I refused to let the pain of my past mar the elegant wooden horse below me, sullying its joyful purpose. The laughter of those around me echoed in the castle courtyard, standing out in strident contrast to what my life had become.

I spent every day in the happiest place on earth, but my happily ever after felt farther away than ever.

Chapter 2

Lucas

I groaned and groped at my phone haphazardly until I silenced the sound of every hard-working dwarf and the too-cheery Heigh-Hos that had interrupted my glorious sleep. Through sleep-filled eyes, I squinted at the time, and let out another groan when 5:31 AM winked back at me above the snooze button.

Rolling to my back and fixing my gaze on the crack in the ceiling above me, I stretched my arms over my head before scrubbing the fatigue from my face and sitting up to avoid any lingering desire for unconsciousness.

Time to make some magic.

I smiled at my own internal pep talk with the tagline I used with my social media accounts. It was silly and special all at the same time, as it was something my mom used to say to me every time she donned an apron in our sunny yellow kitchen at home. She may have just been an amateur baker, but her strawberry rhubarb pie was absolute perfection.

My mouth watering at the thought of warm, tangy pie, I swung my legs over the side of the bed and came face-to-face with my prized vintage Matterhorn poster, signed by Imagineer and legend Bob Gurr himself. "Good morning, Bob," I said as I grabbed my phone off the nightstand and moved towards the kitchen to start my day.

As my coffee maker percolated a cup of brew, I scrolled through TikTok, liking and commenting on posts and seeing what the algorithm threw my way. Mostly it was Disney, of course, with some random trending videos thrown in the mix. Every once in a while a penguin popped up, because, honestly, who can resist a tuxedo-clad penguin? I'd been hooked ever since I saw the ones dancing with Bert in Mary Poppins.

I prepped my coffee and carried it to my small balcony, stepping out into the sunshine as I took in the Anaheim skyline. It wasn't much, to be honest, but my view of Guardians of the Galaxy: Mission Breakout made the ridiculous rent of this studio loft worth it. I settled in a worn plastic Adirondack chair that was my happy place away from my happy place and resumed scrolling social, pausing every once in a while to answer people's comments on my content.

I never set out to be an "influencer." I just liked sharing the fascinating history of the Disney parks in a unique way. My first post was just me making a funny joke about how all the chickens were identical on the Pirates of the Caribbean, something I thought surely everyone already knew.

Turned out they didn't.

The post went viral, gaining over three million views in just 48 hours. After that, with every post, my account grew exponentially, so much so that, two years later, I was able to only work a part-time gig as an event videographer and focus more on being right where I belonged.

That is, walking right down the middle of Main Street, USA.

Well, maybe not *exactly* the middle. My ankles don't have a trolley-track death wish, after all.

Glancing at the time at the top of my screen, I jumped up and started moving. I was within walking distance of the parks, but I still hadn't showered or picked out my Disney bounding outfit for the day.

Fifteen minutes later, I was making my way toward the parks clad in an orange shirt, blue shorts, and a lime-green hat with the word "gawrsh" scrolled across it in an urban font. I usually had standing plans on Tuesday to meet up with my friend Eric, but he had texted me late last night saying he had a chance at a last-minute shoot with a B-list celebrity, and he couldn't pass it up.

I was happy for Eric. He was one of the most talented people I knew, and the best friend a Disney nerd could ever have. It was awesome watching him grow into his own as his career hit its stride.

Eric often reminded me of the Genie from *Aladdin*. He always saw people's worth even when they couldn't see it, whether they were beaten down by circumstances or didn't see the extent of their own value. He had been around through some of my lowest points, reminding me to stay focused on my goals and pulling me out of my own self-pity during the aftermath of a broken heart.

I'll always remember when I told him about the breakup. He simply said, "It's about time" and that I didn't need to change for another person, no matter what they told me I needed to be.

Or what *she* told me I needed to be.

I unzipped my Goofy-themed backpack for security and watched them rifle through my gear, all the while lost in thought. Eric and my regular crew might not be in the parks today, but I had so many friends waiting for me here, all contained in the tiny box in my hand.

Smiling to myself as I walked through the gates, I held up my phone in front of my face and hit the red button to start the live stream.

With each person that joined, my heart felt lighter. Even by myself, I wouldn't be alone.

I had my people.

"Hey there, Disney friends! It's time to make some magic!"

Three hours into my live, I'd already been on the Jungle Cruise, Big Thunder Mountain Railroad, and Mr. Toad's Wild Ride. I'd eaten the new Fly a Kite cupcake at Jolly Holiday Bakery, done a walking tour of New Orleans Square, and shown everyone the newly restored Mary Blair murals in Tomorrowland. All my friends in the live chat, who called themselves the Raven Clan after one of the original Ghost Host concepts of the Haunted Mansion, were voting on what I should do next, and I took a moment to sit down in the circular hub before the castle and just enjoy the view.

Some may say that Disneyland's castle is small and disappointing, but whenever my eyes pass over its turrets and spires, I've only ever seen it as the realization of a dream. Walt must have seemed absolutely crazy to many people as he pitched this idea of an amusement park when, at the time, amusement parks were seen as dirty, crowded places only out to get your money. And putting a big castle in the center just for aesthetics and not even a single thrill ride? What was the point, really?

But Walt had a vision. He could see it. Despite all the naysayers and even when aspects of it were still just a fuzzy long-shot of an idea, he knew what he was building and why, and he never gave up until the dream became reality.

I was determined to do the same.

Stretching my legs in front of me and crossing them at the ankles, I mentally checked back into the chat and saw that everyone had voted for doing the Sleeping Beauty Castle walk-through, followed by Pirates of the Caribbean, and had now moved on to discussing which Pirates movie was the best.

I threw my two cents in the mix (the first one, of course, because they use Marc Davis's "Island of Lost Souls" concept of pirates turning from humans to skeletons) before pushing to stand and striding over toward the right side of the castle. In the chat, several people yelled at me, all in good fun, that I couldn't use concept art to make decisions about the best movie. I shook my head and rolled my eyes. This wasn't the first time I'd had to defend my passion for all things Disney history.

"Of course, I can. And you know what? If Disney made a movie with all their original pirates from the concept art like Sir Francis Verney & Sir Henry Mainwaring, I'd be there in a heartbeat. As it is, we only got Mr. Gibbs from Captain Charles Gibbs and a few murals of all of them in the queue. I mean, come on. Where are the REAL pirates?"

I watched the chat as it started flying, pleased with myself that I'd stirred the pot and that so many people didn't know I was partially kidding. I love the Pirates movies, just as they are. And, truthfully, many of those "real" pirates died in the poor house or of syphilis from the brothels they frequented, so their stories weren't exactly destined for the silver screen.

Just then, one of my moderators and good friends popped up in the chat to chime in.

Ms.Pixiedst: *no pirate will ever be better than Captain Jack Sparrow*

"Ha! Well, we can all agree on that Pixie, 100 percent. He may not be original to the attraction, but he is iconic in his own right."

I paused as I crossed the bridge to Snow White's fountain and panned my phone over the magical nook tucked to the right of the castle that many people tended to overlook. Every fifteen minutes, the fountain came to life with spinning fish and a wishing well that echoes Snow White's "I'm Wishing" song.

I took a deep breath and launched into one of my favorite Disney tales:

"You know, a long time ago, we all believed that these white marble sculptures of Snow White and the Seven Dwarfs were a gift from an Italian sculptor who used a set of European soaps as his model to carve the statues, which made him accidentally create them all the same size since that's how they fit into the box. Then, as the story goes, John Hench came up with the idea to put Snow White up at the top of the fountain to make her look like she is the correct size compared to her dwarf friends, using—"

"—Using forced perspective to correct the artist's mistake."

I looked to my right, startled at the interruption.

"But a few years ago," said a young woman, continuing my story, "they found something in John Hench's desk. Right there was the evidence that he himself had made a mistake converting the measurements, and that's why they are the same size."

She was exactly right, of course.

And that was the moment I found my new dream.

Chapter 3

Leah

I grinned up at him, this mysteriously handsome brown-haired, blue-eyed stranger who knew my story, and told it even better than I could.

"What, you think a girl can't know her Disney history?" I tossed out playfully.

The stranger blinked, his mouth agape. He cleared his throat a few times, seeming to shake himself out of his shock before responding.

"Uh, no, I mean, yes, I mean.... Hi. I'm Lucas, aka LucaDisNerd" He stuck out a hand for me to shake, and I slid my own into his, giving it a firm up and down.

"Hey, I'm Leah, LeahMetotheMagic. I haven't seen you around before, are you here often?"

I let go of his hand and glanced at my live stream, the chat flying with questions, asking who we were talking to and if they could see him. Someone said he sounded hot, and I could feel myself blushing, knowing he could see my screen from the way the phone was angled currently at the fountain. I tilted it slightly away from his view.

"Yeah, I'm here five days a week," he replied. "I'm surprised I've never run into you either. Do you stream a lot?"

I froze. I knew he was just being friendly. I had just asked him this same question, for churro's sake. But there was always that part of me that was scared, that knows how sharing information can be dangerous with the wrong person.

But, then again, he could easily see my live streams anytime now that he knew my account name.

How could I be so careless? He could find me whenever he wanted to now. And I don't even know him.

I could feel the panic rising, but then I glanced in his direction. He was simply smiling and making jokes about the fountain, looking relaxed.

Happy.

Maybe even ... safe.

But no. Once, I had thought *he* was safe too.

Still, I was safe here, in this place. I could be friendly. It wouldn't hurt.

I hoped.

Just as I took a deep breath to ease away the anxiety, I heard him describing me to his followers.

"Oh, I just met her. No, we've never seen each other before. Yeah, she does sound nice."

Then, turning to me and looking sheepish, "Hey, are you ok if I show you on camera? Some people are asking…"

"Oh!" I responded. "Oh, of course! And my people are asking too—to see you."

"Not much to see, but totally," he joked with a grin.

We stepped a few feet away from each other on the bridge with pink hearts engraved on the woodwork and pointed our phones in each other's direction. It gave me an excuse to really take in his whole physique, noticing his tall frame and hilariously subtle "Goofy" Disneybound.

The people in my chat noticed, too.

DisneeLuv23: Well, hello, Prince Charming!

KyloFanGirl100: Can we take him home?

MinnieMags: Girl, was he telling your Snow White statue story? We need more information!

There were also a record number of hearts flying across the screen, all triggered by Lucas who was now giving me ridiculous over-the-top model poses while I just stood there and smiled and waved to his crew. After our people had gotten their fill, we stepped toward each other again, turning our phones back to the fountain.

"So... how do you know about the statues?" I asked, turning my head in his direction and smiling.

"Oh, you know, word, gets around. I love to read, and I know a few people who know some insider information. You?"

"Same. Are you into park history much?"

Lucas laughed out loud, his voice booming across the water and thawing a piece of my heart I didn't realize was frozen. It was refreshing to hear a man laugh in such a genuine way, not in derision or because he knew he had the upper hand.

"You could say that," Lucas replied "I have only been obsessed with it ever since I was ten and realized the planter in Mr. Toad's Wild Ride queue was only there because of—"

"—the skyway tower! YES! Oh my goodness, I can't believe you know that! Nobody knows that!" I exclaimed excitedly, turning toward him in disbelief.

Lucas was looking at me, grinning from ear to ear.

"Wow, I didn't know anyone else knew that either. Guess it was meant to be that we'd find each other. I mean, that we'd meet up. Uh, I mean... um..."

My eyes widened as he desperately tried to backpedal out of the awkwardness. My chat flew with variations of "What did he say?, OMG MARRY HIM," & "He really *is* Prince

Charming." I knew he had just misspoken, so I didn't think anything of it, but he looked so stricken that I decided to step in and save the day.

"I know what you meant, no worries! Hey, do you want to go on a ride together? Maybe we can see what other crazy Disney history we both know."

Looking visibly relieved, he let out a long breath. "Absolutely I do."

I smiled at his subtle reference to *The Office*. "Okay, where to?"

"Well, I was headed to the castle walkthrough, but everyone is telling me in the chat that they want me to skip it and go to Pirates. Are you game?"

My inner Disney nerd rejoiced. Pirates of the Caribbean was my second favorite ride, only after the Haunted Mansion, and there was so much history and so many facts to share with my online friends.

"Let's do it," I responded. I felt slightly nervous to go on a dark ride with a stranger, but knowing we were both live streaming and that the Disney cameras were watching (or, as Roz from *Monster's Inc* would say, "always watching"), I felt confident that one ride wouldn't hurt.

And there was something about Lucas. The way he moved, the way he smiled ... it just made me feel lighter, like someone had secretly attached the balloons from *Up* to my backpack. He was free in a way that I didn't know how to be anymore.

But I wanted to be.

As I strolled through Frontierland a few minutes later keeping pace with my newfound Disney history nerd friend, I kept one eye on my chat while listening to the comments he was throwing out to his own audience here and there.

"You know, the *Mark Twain* actually runs faster than the *Lilly Belle* in the Magic Kingdom. This steamboat moves at a pace of 2.0 knots, while the *Lilly Belle* only goes 1.6. I guess you could say it's 'k-n-o-t' as fast."

My head swiveled in his direction, and my eyes widened before a ridiculous laugh tripped its way out of my mouth. I was startled by it, the sound of it so foreign to my ears. I hadn't had anything to laugh about in a long time, but for some reason, the ridiculously bad joke caught me off-guard.

Lucas pulled his focus from his screen and smiled at me as his long legs strode beside mine.

"What? Was that k-n-o-t funny? I *ashore* you, people are laughing in my chat. I'm a funny guy, and *schooner* or later you were bound to find out."

That's all it took for me to completely lose it. I committed the number one Disney parks sin and stopped in the middle of the walkway without warning, doubling over in laughter. Tears trickled and then started streaming down my face, and I gasped for breath between bursts of hysterical laughter. People flooded by and gave me annoyed looks as they dodged and weaved around us.

Pausing next to me and patiently waiting for my sanity to return, Lucas playfully narrated my lunacy for all his viewers.

"We interrupt this journey to the Caribbean to bring you LeahMetotheMagic, who is currently trying to breathe after witnessing the glory that is my humor and presence. She'll be throwing tomatoes by this time tomorrow, no doubt, like you all do after hearing these same corny jokes a million times. But for now, let's all marvel at Princess Leah losing it in front of the wildest ride in the wilderness."

My laughter stopped abruptly, with a hiccup and a sudden intake of breath.

Did he just call me—

No. He wouldn't know what that means to me. How could he know?

"Why… why did you call me that?" I said softly as my mind reeled with the sudden hard shift of my train of thought. I was suddenly transported years earlier, to a bittersweet memory of the last time that name was spoken to me.

Why did grief have to linger so long and hurt so much?

Every so often, a reminder of just how much I'd lost surprised me by showing up as subtly as the pop-up ghosts that used to be in the attic of the Haunted Mansion, catching me off-guard every time.

How was I supposed to explain this to Lucas?

Lucas furrowed his brow and cocked his head with concern, clearly wondering what he had said to upset me. My mind started to race, instantly switching into the fight-or-flight response that had become my best friend in social settings during the past year.

Great, Leah, way to go. He's clearly trying to figure out if I'm actually a lunatic, and probably reconsidering meeting me at all. Maybe I should just say my goodbyes. This was a mistake. I don't even know him. I shouldn't have said anything, I should have just—"

"What… Princess Leah? Was that not ok?"

My heart broke a little when a puzzled look settled onto his face. I hated knowing that my messed-up self had put it there.

He didn't know how truly broken I was. If he had, he'd make a polite but hasty exit back to Fantasyland where everyone and everything has a happy ending, running away as fast as he could from me and my Mr. Toad existence. Lucas didn't need a wild ride that would inevitably end in tragedy, and that's all I had to offer.

I squeezed my eyes tightly closed as tears of embarrassment burned behind them, threatening to show more than I wanted anyone to see. I never broke down in front of anyone like this. And especially never on a live stream, because *he* could be watching, and I don't let him see me fall apart.

Not anymore.

My eyelids popped open, immediately taking in my surroundings and assessing my safety out of habit, reassuring myself he wasn't here. My frantic, seeking gaze didn't reveal anything dangerous but instead landed on a pair of kind, cobalt-blue eyes regarding me with quiet concern.

Lucas.

Lucas, who'd been watching me carefully, observed my countenance shifting from mirth to something else entirely.

Lucas, who seemed to see more of me than I had offered to him, more than most people would care to see, and yet he was still there.

Lucas, who was not running.

Instead, this stranger I met just a handful of minutes ago miraculously jumped into action. He somehow must have sensed I was paralyzed and hopped in front of my phone, addressing my live audience and his own simultaneously.

"Hey everyone, we're going to take a quick break before Pirates to get some O2H. We'll be back in a few!"

He met my gaze as he pronounced each word, silently inquiring with a quirked brow if that was what I needed. I gave him a small nod, and he reached out, tapped my screen, and ended my live before doing the same to his own. My hand and my phone fell to my side.

Lucas took a few steps toward me, coming closer to hide our words from the river of people who flowed by us, creating our own private island despite my numbness and his awkward confusion.

Hesitantly, he stretched out a hand and laid it on my shoulder, a simple offer of comfort that both terrified and thrilled me all at once.

I shivered.

When was the last time I let anyone get this close?

When you let him make you into someone you're not.

I cleared my throat and tried to salvage this social trainwreck of a meeting with this perfectly innocent bystander who suddenly had a front-row seat to my personal tragedy.

"I'm so sorry. It's nothing, it's just ..."

"Hey. It's ok. You don't have to say anything. Let's go sit down in the shade for a few, ok?"

I took a deep breath, the air shuddering in my lungs as the aftermath of my held-back tears made itself known. I needed to find a way out of this. Lucas probably had plans that didn't include my pathetic self.

I needed to save him from my reality.

I started to babble, so far from my comfort zone that it was like being in a Disney parking lot when you'd forgotten where you parked the car. My eyes bounced from the Golden Horseshoe to the petrified tree to a couple wearing matching Mickey & Minnie t-shirts and everywhere in between. Anywhere and everywhere but at the stranger who must be thinking I was absolutely crazy by this point.

"You don't have to do this. I'll be fine. Really. You go ahead to Pirates. I'll meet up with you another time. If you want to, I mean. You don't have to. Not that I think you—"

"Leah."

The way he said my name snapped my gaze to his.

"Come with me," he whispered, giving me a small, reassuring smile and a gentle squeeze on my shoulder before dropping his hand and stepping back, allowing me the choice of whether to follow or not.

I hesitated.

His gaze stayed steady with my own, silently asking me to trust him.

I shouldn't.

I couldn't.

But then Lucas started moving, and something told me if I didn't go with him, I'd regret it.

So I went, keeping pace with him as we carefully picked our way through the crowds, his arm occasionally brushing my own as the crowds jostled us. My heart was racing because I knew this was risky. Everything in me said I should run, and fast, as far away from Lucas as possible. And yet, as he turned to look at me and offered a shy smile of encouragement, I had no thought of running.

No, I only wanted to stay. And that was what scared me the most.

Chapter 4

Lucas

I saw the panic in Leah's eyes the instant my hand settled on her shoulder in my awkward attempt to comfort her.

I don't know what made me do something so familiar with someone I just met, but there was something about Leah that begged for connection, especially as I watched the shimmer in her eyes shape-shift from tears of joy to those of pain.

Something was wrong with Leah, and I wasn't about to let her just walk away, especially if I could help.

I led Leah onto the porch that wrapped around the Golden Horseshoe, leaving behind the buzz and whirlwind of the major thoroughfare in favor of a little-used nook in the back corner under the overhang.

Conscious of how I'd already toed the line of her personal space, I left room between us as we came to a halt before a weathered wooden bench. We both took a seat, side by side, looking out at the sun reflecting off the gently rippling water of the Rivers of America.

Leah was quiet.

I waited.

The *Mark Twain* whistled and chugged by as my thoughts centered on the beautiful person next to me, giving her space. I desperately wanted to know what I'd said that made her so upset. I never wanted to repeat such a mistake again.

Leah shifted and sighed.

I waited some more.

A mom walked by with a toddler having a meltdown in a stroller. A couple sauntered around the corner discussing where they should have dinner. Park life moved on around us, but as for me, my whole world had paused. There was only Leah and me and a made-to-look-older-than-it-was bench.

Leah sighed again.

"I'm really sorry."

I turned my head to look at Leah, her shoulders slumped and her eyes focused on her lap as she wrung her hands in a nervous dance.

"What for?"

"For … all of it. For getting emotional, for being a complete lunatic. It's not at all like me to do that, especially not in front of a virtual stranger. I'm sorry I made you ditch your live. I'm sorry I made everything awkward and weird."

I took all this in, turning it around in my head. Leah still wouldn't look at me, shifting her gaze up but in the opposite direction from me, watching everything and nothing at the same time.

I shifted my body to angle toward her.

"Leah. Look at me."

She responded by dropping her gaze back down, clearly embarrassed and not ready to do what I asked. A few soft sniffs gave away the truth, evidence of tears that she struggled to hold back, and my heart squeezed, wishing I could do something, anything, to take away her pain.

I tried again.

"Leah, please look at me?"

My soft pleading drew her chin in my direction, her eyes finally locking on my own.

I spoke slowly and carefully, needing her to hear every word.

"I am no stranger, Leah. I'm Lucas. A fellow Disnerd, wannabe Disney historian, and now a friend. And your being 'emotional' is the most beautiful, real, and honest thing I've seen from any Disney creator in a long time. You don't need to hide it from me. Not ever."

A single tear finally made its way down Leah's cheek. I impulsively reached over and slowly swiped it off her soft skin with my thumb as if it was the most natural thing in the world. Her eyes widened and I heard her breath hitch.

She thought I was going to kiss her.

And I thought I might, too.

My heartbeat accelerated and adrenaline started racing through my body at the thought of pressing my lips to hers.

But then common sense reared its ugly head, and I caught myself.

What was I doing? I didn't even know Leah, not really. We just met. We're not anywhere near finishing each other's sandwiches or anything. Yet.

I smiled at the silly thought, shaking my head. Leah blinked and leaned back a bit, my actions effectively breaking the odd trance we seemed to have been in.

"It was my nickname," Leah suddenly blurted out.

I wasn't following, still lost in my thoughts of Hans and Anna. "What was?"

"Princess Leah. My mom and dad used to call me that back before... before they passed. They were huge Star Wars fans, and they named me after Princess Leia."

I froze. No way.

"Wow."

"What? There's nothing wrong with Star Wars," Leah retorted indignantly, her eyebrows drawing together in consternation.

I shook my head. "No, what I mean is, your parents weren't the only ones with the idea to name their kid after Star Wars."

"Wait ... Lucas. George Lucas?"

"Yup. Well, my full name is actually Lucas Barsotti, but yeah. George Lucas."

"Wow."

"Hey, you stole my line," I accused with a grin.

"That's crazy. Wow. You must really love the original Star Tours queue then."

Her statement pulled a deep laugh out of the core of my being. I'd never met someone who knew about that.

"Where they had an announcement for Endor passenger 'Sacul Egroeg?' Hardly anyone knows about that announcement," I paused. "You're amazing."

Leah beamed, and it was like the sun had come out for the first time. I was left speechless as I studied the new dimple that had just joined us. I was so taken with it that I missed what she was saying, tuning in to hear only, "...Don't you think?"

"Huh?"

Leah gave me a look of mild exasperation.

"I said, don't you think it's time we joined our pirate crew? 'Dead men tell no tales,' and all that?"

I gave myself a mental shake.

Right.

The live.

My work.

Leah, though.

Princess Leah.

My Princess Leah.

Because now there was no doubt in my mind—she was meant for me.

As we passed under the arched bridge that marked the entrance into the Pirates of the Caribbean, my mind was a jumbled mess. I restarted my live and greeted my online friends as their names popped up on my screen, but my heart and soul were still sitting back on that bench in Frontierland, marveling at the unbelievably rapid shift in my world.

Leah was next to me, also back on her live, explaining the history of the bridge and how it was added to increase traffic flow into the New Orleans area. Luckily, my friend Ian (aka DisHistorIan) was in my chat and was giving his own facts about the attraction, like how the costumer Alice Davis made a double set of costumes without telling anyone because the bookkeepers said they couldn't afford two sets. Then, when there was a fire in the attraction, they were both astonished and relieved when she revealed the second set that allowed them to reopen the attraction in a matter of days. All of his storytelling gave me a moment to guide my thoughts back to a place of relative sanity.

Well, mostly. Because when the line started to move and Leah was distracted by the ironwork on the railing, it took everything I had not to put my hand on her lower back to remind her that the line was moving forward. It felt so instinctual that I had to press my hand against my thigh to keep myself within what was acceptable for a human who just met another human.

Even though I was usually a fairly physical person, I didn't want to make Leah uncomfortable if she was not the same way. And while she was cordial and teasing, she definitely gave off a no-touch kind of vibe with the way she held herself. Almost as if she was uncomfortable in her own skin, and was trying hard to make sure the world didn't notice her.

But I noticed her.

Her golden blonde hair that shimmered in the sun.

Her bright green eyes, which seemed to know me when they looked my way.

Her heart-shaped face and soft curving features.

Her.

I sighed, chastising myself. I needed to think of something else, *anything else*, but the woman standing next to me as we inched our way forward to Lafitte's landing. Having just entered the indoor part of the queue, I took a deep breath and inhaled the scent of bromine from the water lapping against the moving boats. It was better than any essential oil, the familiar scent grounding me and reminding me of who I needed to be, and why.

But the hypnotic lap of the waves also drew me in, transporting me to a time when I was standing in this spot with Sadie. She was doing something on her phone as I tried to tell her about how Pirates was originally going to be a walk-through wax museum. I was describing all the different vignettes of the exhibit when she turned to me with a look of disgust and uttered the words that still ring in my ears to this day: "Honestly Lucas, no one cares. I know you're a huge Disney adult or whatever, but could you just stop already with the 'fun facts'?"

Those words paralyzed me for years. From that moment, I mentally shoved all my Disney history knowledge in a shoebox under the proverbial bed and tried to forget it was there. I worked on what Sadie called "just being in the moment" at the parks and slowly my truest self got smaller and smaller until I barely recognized myself.

But as I was riding the Haunted Mansion two years later, I noticed that the photos in the corridor of doors were the same as the Hatbox Ghost and the pop-up ghosts in the graveyard, and I started to laugh, maybe a little louder than was appropriate. Sadie tried to shush me, telling me people were looking and I was going to ruin the ride for everyone else.

I just laughed harder at the irony... I was finally materializing, the real me, even more vividly than the ghosts swirling around in the ballroom below. I had been a foolish mortal, indeed, to think that I could ever pretend not to care about the creative detail and history of these parks that I loved.

When we got off the ride, I paused at the railing of the Rivers of America, and asked Sadie, "What do you see?"

She eyed me with suspicion before taking a cursory look around, gesturing to her surroundings as she answered.

"Dirty water, some ducks, and disgruntled people in a canoe who look like they made the biggest mistake of their life."

I shook my head. She didn't get it. But I wanted her to understand. We'd invested in each other, cared for one another.

"No, Sades, what *more* do you see?"

"Um, a boat? An island? I don't know."

I sighed.

"Sadie ... I see a dream fulfilled, and dreams yet to come true. I see hundreds of hours of creativity and tears and labor and teamwork. I see the tiniest details and the big picture, working together harmoniously to give us a feeling of hope and peace in this world that so often gives us the opposite. I see Walt arguing with Joe Fowler about needing a harbor for the boats, and him strolling arm-in-arm with Lillian around Rainbow Ridge in the evenings. I see all of that and more. But you? You don't see it. You don't get it. And I'm starting to realize you never will."

Sadie looked surprised, shocked even. And I could understand why. I had worked hard to give her everything she needed, becoming who she wanted me to be in the process. But I'd had enough of hiding who I was. Tears streamed down my face, knowing what I had to do, even though it killed me to hurt her.

"I love you, Sades. And a part of me always will. But we don't see the world the same way, and I think it would be better if we weren't together anymore."

Sadie was silent, taking it all in. Then she turned to me, her eyes distant and unrecognizable as she coldly said, "You'll never do better than me. I accepted your stupid Disney obsession. I looked the other way as you dressed in all those ridiculous outfits and hats. No one is ever going to want someone like you. You'll see."

And with that, she walked out of Frontierland and out of my life forever.

Leah's melodic voice as she narrated to her live stream brought me back to the present, and I realized we were about to load into our bateau.

"Can you imagine? Yale Gracey had never even *seen* a real live firefly before he invented these. He just tinkered around until he made a convincing effect with just a grain of wheat bulb, a wire, and a fan. Brilliant. Absolutely brilliant!"

Leah's whole face was illuminated with joy at the thought of Gracey's creative Imagineering as she looked back at me and grinned.

My heart skipped a beat, and the smile I returned had to have been brighter than the entire sum of all the bulbs in the Main Street Electrical Parade.

She faced forward again and held up two fingers to the Cast Member indicating the size of our party. They saw our live recordings and gestured for the back row of the boat. I was secretly grateful, I'd hate to ruin anyone's ride experience with the lights from our phones, even though I always pulled mine close to my chest and spoke in low tones.

I glanced down at my chat on my live, realizing I hadn't said anything in a while. But it turned out that they hadn't minded; they were listening to Leah and discussing what she had been talking about.

DisHistorIan: *Dude, Lucas, marry that girl.*

Ms.Pixiedst: *She's amazing! I have been taking notes like a crazy person*

user9863572: *I love her, she's so sweet and takes the time to answer everyone's questions*

Andyscoming22: *Is she single? can you ask her for me?*

I bristled at that last comment. I suddenly felt protective of Leah, and as we climbed into our bateau, I wondered at the tinge of jealousy in my heart. It didn't make any sense. I didn't have any right to feel that way about her; she didn't belong to me. We had just met.

My body tensed at the thought that maybe she did have a boyfriend— that I had thought about kissing someone who could be, at this very moment, in a committed relationship.

My stomach tightened.

I had to know.

But being on a live, there wasn't much that I could do that my community or hers wouldn't pick up on if I wasn't careful. I needed to be stealthy.

As the bayou embraced us with dancing fireflies and the peaceful calm of a blue-cast twilight, I waited until Leah was done talking about Beacon Joe, who slowly rocked and picked at his banjo on the porch of his small hut. I watched her in my peripheral vision, her hands animatedly flying like Walt's used to, as she told the tale of how Beacon Joe's audio-animatronic was identical to the king in the Haunted Mansion, as well as one of the pirates enticing the dog with the keys at the end of the ride. When she took a breath, I shifted my phone to my left hand and held it away from my body. Then I slid my right arm behind her on the back of the boat, leaning in close to her ear to keep our conversation private.

Startled, Leah leaned away from me at first, turning her head to look into my eyes while a hint of alarm appeared in her own. I tapped my mouth with my index finger and then pointed to her live, and she seemed to understand that I just wanted to speak without being heard. Settling herself facing forward again and pulling her phone away from herself as I did, I leaned back in, feeling my lips just brush a few strands of her hair as I whispered, "So, does your boyfriend like all of these crazy Disney facts, Leah?"

She ducked her head as her gaze shifted to her lap.

At first, I thought maybe she was just shy, or embarrassed. But then I noticed her hand was shaking.

As she slowly raised her head and moved her lips to my ear, I felt as frozen in time as the skull and crossbones we floated closer to every second. Never had I anticipated an answer so desperately.

"No, I ... I don't have a boyfriend."

She paused so long next to my ear, that I thought maybe she had planned to add more, but she pulled back, looking into my eyes in the dim light of the cave as if she was trying to communicate words she couldn't say.

I kept my eyes locked on hers, searching. Wanting to see if there was indeed what I thought there was between us. I felt a little reckless, my whole body wanting to say four simple words that could scare her off forever, but I felt like I'd waited a lifetime to say them.

"Do you want one?" was all set to trip off my tongue, but at that moment our boat decided it was time to fall perilously down two drops in the dark, and the moment slid away with it.

Chapter 5

Leah

It was time.

The exit gates loomed before me as I reluctantly said goodnight to Disneyland along with a few other late-night guests. Colette was with me, the two of us having closed down the park together. Repeating their nightly routine, the line of security guards had slowly but surely moved toward the front of the park, escorting the few remaining guests who had lingered on Main Street back to the entrance into the real world.

"So long, Hank! Thanks for letting us linger, as always. You're the best!" Colette gave him a dazzling smile and a quick salute.

Hank the security guard had become a friend of ours over the months, knowing our routine and trusting that we would follow the rules and do as asked. We respected him and the boundaries Disney had put in place, and he in turn allowed us a few extra moments by the castle here and there when we needed it.

"Hank, how is that new grandbaby treating you?" I asked, knowing how soft the old gruff military vet got when asked about his five grandkids.

The corners of his mouth betrayed a hint of a smile as he no doubt pictured the tiny newborn in his mind. "You know she's sweet as sunshine, Leah. I saw her just yesterday, and she's growin' like a weed!"

I laughed. "Weeds weren't so great in Alice in Wonderland, you know, Hank. Maybe you should find a new analogy."

Hank shook his head. "Ain't nothing better than a baby growin' and growin'. She'll be runnin' circles around me before you know it." And with that, he gestured with one arm toward the gate, kindly letting us know it was time for us to make our way out of the park.

I always melted at the obvious love that radiated from Hank when he talked about his family. He was the real deal, a genuine human being who was tough when he needed to be, but deep down he was a big ol' softy with a heart of gold. Hank often looked out for me in the park, knowing that I was usually on my own. If I came close to trusting anyone, it was Hank. I knew he had my back.

"Have a good night, Hank! See you tomorrow!" I tossed him a small wave and a smile. Beside me, Colette said her own goodbyes as well.

Hank sent us off as he always did. "Be safe, girls."

Colette and I walked with weary feet out of the gates and through the empty plaza. I always made sure to end my live before heading home, knowing that *he* was watching.

Max.

I didn't want him to know when I left and where I went after. Not to mention a thousand other crazies on the internet who had a tendency to stalk me if they knew where I was. In the parks was one thing but out here? No thanks.

"Sooooo Leah …" Colette began, watching me carefully with a sly, knowing smirk. "I saw that you were hanging out with LucaDisNerd on his live earlier today. I didn't know you two knew each other."

I swallowed. My heart rate kicked up a notch at the mention of Lucas. I forced nonchalance into my tone as I answered, "Yeah, we bumped into each other by the castle. He was talking about the Snow White statues, telling one of my favorite stories. He knows as much as I do, if not more, about Disney history. He's amazing."

Colette was uncharacteristically quiet for a minute as we strolled toward Harbor Boulevard together under the dim yellow lights.

"Leah, can I ask you something?"

I instantly tensed. I could sense this wasn't going to be an easy question, and I hated lying to my friend, especially one who was so loyal and kind, even if she was a bit crazy at times.

"Of course, Col. Ask away," I ground out with the world's fakest smile.

She eyed me with suspicion but continued on anyway. She wasn't known to mince words, and I loved that about her. Usually.

"Are you ever going to tell me what really happened to you? Because if you can't even tell me the truth, how are you going to get involved with someone like Lucas? He's a decent guy, and he deserves better than that. You know I adore you, and I put up with your secrets because I think you need me to, but that's not fair to ask of someone you're seeing."

My jaw clenched. She saw so much more than I realized. And instantly I was on the defensive, crossing my arms over my chest.

"Who said I'm seeing him? I saw him *once*, Col. *Once*. We hung out. Like you did with... what's his name? Oh yeah, EricOnTheHunt. How's that going, by the way? You married yet?"

Her face turned bright red, and I knew I'd gone too far. Regret enveloped me as I watched her crumble and turn inward right before my eyes. I knew I should have said something, anything, to pull all my words back and be the friend she deserved, but the broken part of me didn't know how. Her voice was smaller with her response, and I cringed at knowing I was the one who had made it that way.

"I'm going to let that slide. You know how I feel about Eric and why we can't ... why I can't ... just..." She looked away from me, and I wondered if I shouldn't be cast as the next great Disney villain, considering how callous I'd been in the face of her vulnerability.

Some friend I was. They say that hurt people *hurt people*, and I was the poster child for doing just that. I sighed and tugged on her arm, turning her to face me in the empty plaza between the parks where, ironically, *Toy Story's* "You've Got a Friend in Me" was playing from the hidden speakers.

"I'm so sorry Col. I know better. I know how you feel about Eric and I messed this up. I ... am scared. I don't know what to do with Lucas. He's like ... *me*. But a me that isn't scarred and jaded. He seems so lighthearted and unapologetically *free*. I'm worried that I'll ..." I trailed off, my eyes involuntarily following a tired family's progress as they slowly plodded out the security gates in front of us.

"You'll what, Leah?" Colette prompted softly.

I sighed and looked down at my weary, flip-flop-clad feet. "I'm worried that I'll ruin him. That I'll take all the light and joy that's in him and make it dark," I whispered. I seamed my lips tightly closed against the truth that begged to slip out, that I was wholly unworthy of Lucas, and that letting anyone get too close to me was dangerous because Max was always watching.

And jealous.

He believed me to be his, even now. And he hated anyone touching what was his.

Colette instantly gathered me into her arms in a hug that spoke of a kind of comfort I'd almost forgotten was possible, outside of my Aunt Meredith. Colette understood me, even when I barely gave her enough information to fully understand.

"Lucas would be luckier than the Little Man of Disneyland to have you, my friend," she murmured into my ear, referencing one of my favorite little-known characters, a tiny leprechaun from a 1955 Little Golden Book who was now housed in the base of a tree in Adventureland. After squeezing me tightly for a second, she let go and pulled back, keeping her hands on my arms as she spoke words that I wanted to believe.

"He's a good guy. But you are an extraordinary woman who brings joy and light to everyone you encounter. You can't possibly dim his world; you could only amplify it. You'd be his second star to the right." She grinned at me, adding, "Or, rather, he'd be yours."

I swallowed the lump that had formed in my throat and blinked away the tear that wanted to slide down my cheek. Tentatively, I took hold of the hope my friend gave me and weighed it in my hands. We strolled to the exit, Colette knowing she would have to split off from me once we crossed the street, as usual. I grew silent as we walked and she allowed me my space as I mulled over the words we had shared.

What if she was right?

The idea of being with Lucas made tiny little bread-and-butterflies flit around in my chest, but I shooed them away. I knew who I was and what was at stake for anyone who got too close to me.

I wasn't a safe person. I was an accessory to murder.

And Max wouldn't let me forget it.

Luckily, Lucas wasn't interested in me anyway; he was just polite and friendly. Not to mention unbelievably kind, especially to someone who was being so ridiculously emotional with someone they just met. I almost groaned aloud at the memory of how I'd shut down in front of him, and how he had to come to my rescue on my live stream.

But then I remembered the scent of Lucas as he leaned in close to me on Pirates, like warm sunshine and an ocean breeze. I thought of how he had softly inquired if I had a boyfriend. And how he grinned at me like I was a rare character sighting when I talked about how Marc Davis never liked going up the waterfall at the end of Pirates of the Caribbean—something Walt had wanted.

He had finished my story, explaining that in the Walt Disney World version, you get out in the basement and take a moving speed ramp uphill instead, because Marc Davis was in charge, and he planned to use the "upward waterfall" idea in a better way in the Western River Expedition ride which he had still hoped to build.

And that was when I knew I was in trouble.

I looked over my shoulder once, twice, then once more just before I slid the key into the lock of the darkened lobby. Seeing no one, I twisted the key and slid the automatic door just wide enough for my Loungefly-clad body to squeeze through before yanking out the key and quickly shutting the door shut behind me. I flipped the inner lock in place and leaned against the door, breathing a sigh of relief.

Safe.

I texted Colette, letting her know I'd made it home without incident. Not that she knew where my home was; I made sure she was well out of sight before ducking into the lobby of the newly-refurbished Cabana Inn. As much as I trusted Colette, I didn't ever want to put her in danger, and if she knew where I lived, it left her vulnerable.

I shuddered at the thought of Max and what he would do to Colette to get to me.

Moving away from the automatic doors, I proceeded into the lobby and behind the counter, inhaling the lingering scent of my Aunt Meredith's chocolate chip cookies along the way. It was a tradition for her to make them every afternoon for her guests, and I hoped she had left a few for me in my room as she often did.

I glanced at my phone, noting the 1:32 AM time, and tried to move a little more quietly as I shuffled to the hidden apartment behind the desk that Meredith and I shared. It wasn't anything fancy, just a main living space with a tired blue couch, a tiny ancient TV, and a small kitchen, with two doors on one wall, each leading to a bedroom.

Before I arrived, Aunt Meredith used my spare room for yoga/scrapbooking/a-shrine-to-everything-90s, and it hadn't changed much since I didn't really have anything when I arrived. So I slept each night under a poster of Helga and Gerald from *Hey, Arnold!* and retrieved my clothes each morning from a dresser topped with Furbies and Tamagotchies. My heart was full knowing that my delightfully quirky aunt wasn't afraid to love what she loved, no matter what anybody thought of it or how out of fashion it might be.

I slipped quietly past Meredith's door and into my room, peeling off my park bag and my 75th Anniversary Minnie ears as I gently pushed the door closed behind me.

Toeing off my shoes, I fell back on my bed with a sigh, reveling in how good it felt to be off my feet after so many hours of live streaming. My body ached and my arm felt like jello from holding my phone for so long, but I didn't care. I was safe and I was doing something I loved, every day. That was all I could really ask for.

I hated to move an inch from my supine position, but I felt every microgram of park grime all over me and knew I had to have a shower before completely calling it a night. With a groan, I pulled myself to sitting, gathered some clean pajamas, and plodded towards the shared bathroom just off the main living space. Luckily I had mastered the art of quick late-night, post-park showering, so I was soon donning my soft classic Mickey tee and black sleep shorts and sliding under the sheets, thankful for the exhaustion that made sleep come so easily despite all the thoughts that liked to creep into my mind in the dark.

I plugged in my phone on my nightstand, clicked off the light, and sank into my pillow with a deep, contented sigh, sure of a solid night of sleep.

Except it never came.

Because all I saw when I closed my eyes was Lucas.

Lucas, oblivious to my presence as I watched him animatedly explain about the Snow White grotto.

Lucas, the way he looked at me on the bench with heartbreaking compassion he didn't owe a complete stranger.

Lucas, as he leaned close to me in the dark and whispered a simple question in my ear that I still heard echoing in my heart.

"Does your boyfriend like all of these crazy Disney facts, Leah?"

He wouldn't ask me that if he wasn't ... *interested* in me like that. Right?

Frustrated with myself for having a glimpse of hope I had no right to hold on to, I flipped over to my side and jerked the covers up to my chin.

But the thoughts simply followed me to the other side of my pillow.

I remembered the way Lucas smelled, like a warm summer day. Like the beach trips I used to take with my mom, hunting for sand dollars. Back when life was simple. Easy. Back when the ocean surf would chase us as we ran away squealing, the water always predictably coming and going, in and out. Back when I was loved, just as I was.

Tears burned behind my eyes as I remembered her, my mother. She was a vibrant, light-hearted being who radiated kindness and compassion. And she loved to laugh. Sometimes I could still hear her bubbly laughter echoing in my mind, reminding me of the absence of it all too much, now that I'd never hear it again.

She loved Disney and my Dad, in that order. Dad was the one who made her laugh the most, never missing an opportunity for a corny dad joke. I remembered watching them slow dance in the kitchen to vintage records from the 1940s, my mom throwing her head back and laughing hysterically as Dad told her joke after joke until she begged him to stop, tears of mirth flowing down her face as he spun her in circles.

They loved each other wholeheartedly. They didn't have much, but they had each other. And I chose to remember them that way, not as I last saw them, with flashing ambulance lights, crumpled metal, and my aunt squeezing my 9-year-old self tight to her side while telling me over and over that everything would be okay.

Looking back, I think she was trying to convince herself of that, more than simply trying to comfort me. She lost her sister that day.

I lost everything.

My parents, my home, my life as I knew it.

Gone in an instant, because someone wasn't paying attention to the sign that said "One Way."

I flipped to my other side, sighing and squeezing my eyes tighter, remembering how lost I was after that. Aunt Meredith did her best to provide a home and all the love a girl could ask for, but I still felt empty. Alone.

Until *Max*.

I let him in, a whirlwind romance I didn't see coming. He walked into the coffee shop where I worked one day, tall and dark and all kinds of handsome in a dark gray perfectly tailored suit. I was working at the register, and when I asked him what he wanted, he answered, "A large Americano, a blueberry scone, and *you*."

I laughed it off, sure he was just flirting as so many guys do with baristas. I finished his order, and he collected his coffee, but he never left the cafe even when his drink was well past finished. He kept diligently working on his laptop, but glancing my way every once in a while and catching my eye, giving me a curious, knowing half-smile.

I felt equally flattered and nervous at the attention, my mind only half-aware of the orders I took and the drinks I created. As closing time came, I wandered over to his table with a broom in hand, letting him know that it was time to go. He nodded, closed his laptop, and slid it into his bag. Then, as he hiked the strap onto his shoulder, he gave a visual sweep of me from head to toe and inquired, "So, where are we going?"

I was shocked. I stuttered, tripping over my words to explain I didn't mean "we" were going anywhere, that it was just time for the cafe to close. He grinned and stepped close to me, a predatory look on his face, before simply stating, "I know."

I breathed a sigh of relief.

But then he added, "So, where are we going, beautiful?"

He pulled the broom out of my shocked hands and leaned it against a nearby chair, gently grabbing hold of my shoulders and rotating my body away from him. I was frozen in place and became hyper-aware of his spicy cologne as he stepped in so close behind me that the heat of his body radiated into my own.

My brain screamed *run!* My heart ceased to beat as I was equally charmed and terrified by this sudden change in events.

My coworker Mandy slowed her wiping down of the espresso machine behind the bar, observing the scene with wide eyes, as shocked as I was at his bold behavior. Likely, she was weighing whether or not she needed to contact building security. As I started to turn back around, searching for the words to communicate to this stranger that I wasn't available, that he needed to leave, I felt his hands gently graze my hips before lightly sliding across to the tie of my apron sitting on my lower back. Alarm bells rang in my head, but I remained inexplicably frozen in place. I felt intoxicated.

He leaned in closer, sharply tugging on the strings to loosen the bow. His hot breath next to my ear made my knees weak as he rumbled, "I told you I wanted *you*. And I'm not leaving without my full order."

With that, the stranger pulled my apron over my head, tossed it on the counter, and grabbed my hand, striding confidently towards the door as I stumbled along behind, stunned.

With a simple hand lifted in a goodbye gesture to Mandy, he led me out the door and into a dream.

Life was never the same after that. I fell hard, head over heels for this mysterious stranger who lavished me with attention and wanted to know about every detail of my life.

He made me feel wanted, talking about our future, the perfect family we'd have, and the beautiful life we'd build together. It felt like my happily ever after had finally arrived, and I reveled in the feeling of finally belonging with someone again.

My hope was what made me blind to who Max really was, my desperate love for him blurring reality. And so I didn't notice when my fantastic dream started slipping into a nightmare.

By the time I did, it was too late.

I sat up in my bed, breathing heavily and trying to shut down the parts of my brain that were spiraling with the memories of what he did. What he made me into.

I told myself the familiar words again. That I was safe. In control. That he couldn't find me here.

None of it was enough.

I reached for my phone, desperately needing a distraction, and opened my favorite social media app. Before I even knew what I was doing, I typed the name that felt like an escape from all of my chaos into the search bar:

LucaDisNerd

His profile was at the top of the list, and I immediately tapped his name to visit his channel, shaking off the voices in my mind that were screaming at me that this was what stalkers did. I started binging his content, only liking one here and there so he wouldn't be able to tell I had been watching literally everything he'd ever made. His content was brilliant, equal parts funny and insightful, yet I found myself studying his face more than listening to his words. I felt waves of peace wash over me as I watched this extraordinary man speak so passionately and joyfully about my favorite place on Earth.

I tried my hardest to ignore the way my heart tripped every time his eyes connected with me on the other side of the screen.

It didn't mean anything, really, I assured myself. Just a little infatuation with a handsome guy.

But the next morning, I woke up with my phone on my chest where it had fallen and realized that if I wasn't careful, I would fall just the same.

Chapter 6

Lucas

I woke up and blinked at the front of my phone, seeing an unusual number of notifications for six in the morning. I pulled myself to sitting, running a hand over my face to wipe the sleep away and make sense of what I was seeing.

It was then I realized who the notifications were from.

LeahMetotheMagic had liked 84 of my posts.

Eighty-four.

And the sweetest notification: One direct message, from Leah herself.

LeahMetotheMagic: Hey, stranger. Just wanted to say thank you for yesterday. I promise I'm not some super emotional girl who cries at the drop of a hat, I usually reserve that for fireworks and the end of Snow White's Enchanted Wish ;-) Your content is great, I hope to see you again soon!

All the breath went out of my lungs. *She loved my content.* And she wanted to see me again. I couldn't think of a better way to wake up than that.

I let out a whoop and practically leaped out of bed, whistling Zip-a-dee-doo-dah as I started my morning routine. I couldn't shake Leah from my mind. She was there as I poured my coffee, toasted my bagel, watered my pet philodendron named Walt, and picked out my outfit for the day. The soft blue Firehouse Five Plus Two shirt was one of my favorites, and I smiled to myself while not-so-secretly hoping Leah would see it.

I knew she was one of the few people who would understand the reference to the early Disneyland singing group made up of Disney animators.

I grabbed my coffee and my phone and practically danced my way to Disney California Adventure, hopping on my live stream and hoping the elation I felt wasn't obvious to all my online friends.

Much to my chagrin, I wasn't very good at hiding it.

Ms. Pixiedst: *someone must have had some extra churros with his breakfast*

Iwantcastles55: *no kidding, I feel breathless just trying to keep up*

HenryAroundtheWorld: *I don't know where he got this energy from, but I need some over here*

DressingDapperly: *I love his smile today, it's giving me life*

I took a deep breath and tried to slow down my pace and my words, not wanting to reveal what was actually elevating my steps. I had the same feeling that I did when I came around the bend on Radiator Springs Racers to see the magnificent cascading waterfall pouring down the Cadillac Range.

All morning long, thoughts of Leah echoed in my mind, swirling around like the waltzing ghosts in the Haunted Mansion ballroom. I remembered how she looked at me with such trust in her eyes as she explained why calling her "Princess Leah" had upset her so much. I remembered the warmth of her palm as I took her hand, the way she tucked her hair behind her ear when she was nervous, the light that sparkled in her eyes when she talked about Walt's vision for Disneyland and how his success defied the odds.

I pulled my focus back to my audience, knowing that they deserved my full attention and that while Leah was gorgeous and brilliant, I needed to concentrate on the task at hand. Winding my way around the crowds, I stepped out of the main path into Radiator Springs, pointing out details as I sauntered down the street.

"If you look in this window of the Cozy Cone, you can see Buzz Lightyear under the traffic cone."

I ducked into the Cozy Cone Motel to take a quick peek at the menus in the snack windows. There was a new Italian gelato in the colors of the Italian flag for Luigi's home country, a chocolate sandwich cookie shaped like a tire with vanilla ganache rims, and a miniature racetrack piped onto a sugar cookie with tiny gummy cars to race around it. The sunshine warmed my skin as the morning cloud cover burned away and the scent of fresh popcorn drifted through the air from the Popcone booth, tempting me to get some for a snack.

MinnieMags: *my kids would LOVE that racetrack cookie*

MsPixiedst: *I wish I could eat gelato through the screen. And that miniature flag was adorable!*

User8937982678: *Do you know any other fun facts about Radiator Springs, Lucas?*

"Do I know any more fun facts about Disney? Is the Matterhorn Majestic? Of course, I do!"

I walked over to Radiator Springs Curios, my phone swaying on my trusty gray gimbal with each step, stabilizing the motion for my viewers. "See the neon Catmull Oil sign at Lizzie's? Dr. Ed Catmull was president of both Walt Disney Animation and Pixar Studios. Without him, computer-generated animation wouldn't be what it is today."

After giving my followers a full tour of the area, I gave into the temptation for flavored popcorn from the Popcone and sat down on a bench on the main drag to enjoy the bacon cheddar goodness. Removing my phone from my gimbal, I propped it up on my backpack and let the Raven Clan people watch as I rested my arms after holding my phone for so many hours. To my right, the lone traffic light blinked slowly again and again in an endless cycle. I was studying it intently to see if every third blink was slower when someone suddenly flew onto the bench next to me and startled me out of my hazy musing.

When I turned sharply towards my unexpected seatmate, my heart lifted faster than the seats of Soarin's gliders. The person who I'd woken up to, who had elevated my whole morning, was sitting beside me as if it was the most natural thing in the world.

"Helloooo, LucasDisNerd. Imagine seeing you here."

Leah's mischievous grin was so marvelous that I lost all capacity for speech and coherent thought. Her hair caught the sunlight as she tossed it over one shoulder and cocked her head at me, her phone aimed in my direction as she live streamed.

Say something. Don't just stare at her like a creeper.

I cleared my throat and sat up straighter, recovering from seeing the object of my every thought materialize before me, looking even more radiant than I remembered.

"Hey Leah, hey everyone!" I give a lame little wave, all the while berating myself that *that* was all I could come up with.

Out of the corner of my eye, I saw everyone in my chat catching on to Leah's presence.

User2673929: *oooh is that LeahMetotheMagic? I love her streams!*

MagicallyMadebyCourt: *turn us! We want to see her!*

Resortabelle: *Leah is the BEST! I love her content*

DisHistorIan: *Can you ask her where she found that fact about how peter pan's flight was originally going to shoot ping pong balls at you?*

Ms.Pixiedst: *Funny how we would run into her twice in the past two days, hm Lucas?*

I picked up my phone and pointed it in her direction, ignoring Pixie's comment even though it made my heart flip over in my chest.

"Look everyone, it's LeahMetotheMagic! If you're not already following her, RUN to do so right now, I promise you won't regret it! She is a wealth of knowledge about Disney history and the parks, and you will for sure be staying up until the wee hours of the night bingeing her content." I gave Leah a sideways look and a small, knowing wink, letting her know I knew *exactly* what she had been doing last night.

Something about the way she blushed while ducking her head and smiling down at her feet caused me to take it a step further before I stopped to overthink it.

I drifted closer to her ear, facing my phone away from her, as both of us instinctively pulled our listening audience away from ourselves to keep our conversation private.

And then I just said it.

"I woke up to you, Leah. And I loved it."

She gave a small gasp, immediately pulling back to reassure herself of the earnestness that I could feel radiating from my very skin. She found only me, smiling back at her with a lightheartedness I hadn't known was missing in my life. The corner of Leah's mouth lifted with a flirtatious tilt as she leaned in, the heat of her body grazing my arm.

I held my breath, certain my whole world hung on her next hushed words.

"I fell asleep to you, Lucas. And I loved it."

She pulled back, locking her eyes with mine. *Life Could Be a Dream* floated through the air in the dusty Route 66 town around us. Our friends' words flew across our phone screens. A duck waddled under the bench looking for stray popcorn kernels. But neither of us could see anything but each other. The entire world had faded away except for this exquisite creature before me.

I closed the space between us, inching my body closer to hers. I could feel her slight intake of breath, and could practically hear her heart racing at the same pace as mine.

I moved my mouth to the shell of her ear, just letting my lips graze her skin as I whispered six words I hoped she couldn't resist.

"Want some bacon cheddar popcorn, Leah?

Leah burst into laughter, pulling back and catching herself in my unexpected comment. I knew she thought I would say something else, and I wanted to. I really did. But my words for Leah needed to wait for a time that didn't involve the toddler throwing a tantrum two benches down and a hundred tired tourists melting in the sun.

I wanted to be the one to show her just what she deserved. I wanted this more desperately than I'd ever wanted anything. But I didn't want to scare her, and given our interaction yesterday, she seemed to have a past that made her cautious. I wanted to respect that. So I just grinned at her, using humor to prevent myself from revealing feelings she probably wasn't ready for me to hand her just yet.

She recovered from her laughter and took the snack box from my proffered hand.

"I would never say no to sharing your popcorn, Lucas."

She paused for a meaningful second before catching my eyes and repeating a single word under her breath.

"Never."

Call me Prince Charming and get me a glass slipper; this girl was my match in every way.

Leah

Outwardly I was making conversation and acting the part of a put-together-Disney-historian-nerd-live streamer, but on the inside, I was chastising myself for being so forward with Lucas. I had no right, really. I shouldn't have sought him out today or forced him to hang out with me all afternoon. He deserved a perfect girl, one who didn't come with more baggage than Toontown's depot.

But then we took a ride in the swinging cars on the Death Wheel (a.k.a. the Pixar Pal-a-Round Ferris Wheel) and watching him scream like a marmot on high alert brought a lightness to my world that I craved like air. And later, when he matched his stride to mine and was patient to wait with me as I captured the perfect shot for content, or explained some random piece of Disney history, I found myself caring less and less about how he shouldn't be near me. I just stayed in the moment in a way I didn't think was possible anymore.

The sun started to say goodbye to the buildings on Buena Vista Street, bathing each monument to Walt in golden light. It brought a sigh to my lips as I remembered where he had come from, and how he had first arrived in Hollywood as a complete failure. Walt started over again, believing that there was more for him than sadness and struggle.

I wanted to believe that for myself, too.

Lucas and I had just passed through the exit gates of California Adventure when he turned to me with an impish smile fixed on his adorably handsome face.

"Truth or dare, Princess Leah?"

I stopped short, turning towards him. He halted as well, much to the chagrin of the family of four behind us who had to swerve their stroller at the last minute. I grimaced, hating to do that to people, but he had taken me by surprise with his silly request.

"Really, Lucas? Truth or dare?" I rolled my eyes in feigned annoyance, but my upturned mouth betrayed my amusement at his antics.

"Come on. You know you want to. Truth or dare?"

I sighed dramatically. My chat started flying, giving their two cents.

ElsieSnow: *DARE!*

MinnieMags: *dare dare dare*

DizneeLuv23: *Oh it could only be dare*

KyloFanGirl100: *I don't know, dare could be dangerous. It is LUCAS we're talking about here*

AlwzDisneyRdy: *Go with the dare Leah. You won't regret it*

User74873687649382: *truth*

BelleoftheBall78: *Dare!*

WaltInTime: *But he wouldn't be unkind to Leah. I mean, just look at the way he treats her, like a real-life princess*

MinnieMags: *@waltintime Yeah we don't have to worry, he clearly is smitten with her*

I blushed and cleared my throat, angling my screen away from Lucas after noticing the turn of the conversation. The rest of my crew picked up the thread and started speculating, and I was mortified. He was just being kind like he was with anyone. That was all.

He was still looking at me, anticipating my answer.

I took a deep breath. The ambient instrumental version of Under the Sea echoed through the plaza, sounding underwater and far away in my ears as I made the frightening decision to not be the careful, cautious Leah for a moment.

"Dare."

Lucas's whole face lit up with excitement, and I felt both instantly rewarded and terrified. What did he have planned?

"Leah, dear Princess Leah, planned and prepared and always perfect Leah … I dare you, for the first time ever, to *hop* across the plaza, and *only* hop across the plaza. No walking allowed."

I burst out in laughter. "So you're saying you want me to literally *park hop* from California Adventure to Disneyland, in the very sense of the word? Are you crazy?"

"I'm mad as a hatter, Leah. I'm surprised you hadn't picked up on that yet." He grinned down at me." So… what will it be?"

He couldn't be serious. I'd look ridiculous. My stream would bounce like crazy. And all the people around us would be watching.

Lucas was studying my features, no doubt taking in how his absurd proposal wreaked havoc on my well-ordered mind. His eyes softened with understanding, again reading me better than anyone I'd ever known.

"Hey, no worries. I'll do it too. We'll do it together."

With a kind smile, he reached down and took my free hand. My heart felt like it was beating outside my chest, tingles racing up and down my body at the touch. His hand was warm and sure, and instantly I was bolstered into believing I *could* do something wilder than riding on the careening train of Big Thunder Mountain.

"Leah, what's the worst that could happen?"

"I don't know. Being ridiculed by everyone around us? Shamed? Embarrassed? Publicly scorned? Banished from Disney forever and ever, amen?"

Lucas laughed out loud, a joyful sound that radiated through the space between us and buried its way into my very core.

"This plaza is full of Disney adults and little kids. Do you really think they will care?"

I weighed that logic. He made a good point.

I closed up all my misgivings in a box and squeezed his hand a little tighter.

"Ok, let's do it." I flipped my chat screen so it faced toward me for a moment. "Ready for this, Pixie Crew? If you get motion sick, you might not want to watch."

The adrenalin began to pump through my veins in earnest, and I gripped my phone a little tighter in anticipation.

Lucas peeked down at me, his gaze holding mine for a moment as if he was searching for any lingering hesitation. The sun was framed behind his head, giving him an otherworldly glow that felt appropriate for anyone who could actually convince me to do something so foolish. I managed to offer him a smile and a small, reassuring nod.

"On the count of three ..."

I took a deep, centering breath. I could do this.

"One, two, three: GO, GO, GO!"

I kept my feet together as I hopped rapidly across the red pavers below, cackling wildly. Lucas did the same next to me, taking smaller hops than he probably would on his own. Still, with the way I was clinging to him for dear life, it was amazing I wasn't pulling him off balance.

Lucas started shouting encouragement, our phones both bouncing in tandem as our chat screens filled with flying hearts and laughing emojis.

"Almost there, Leah! Come on, just keep hopping, hopping, hopping. What would Walt do? Would he give up? No! Main Street is just ahead! We can do this!"

Tears streamed down my face from my uncontrolled, hysterical laughter. People around us paused to watch the spectacle we were making, but to my surprise, there wasn't a scowl among them. Instead, they formed a human channel of Disney fans for us to travel down, cheering and clapping enthusiastically.

But then suddenly Lucas dropped my hand, and my heart dropped with it.

"Race you to the finish, Leah! First person to the gate wins!"

It took a second for my heart to recognize his move as faith in me and not abandonment. He was encouraging me to be confident, showing me that I could do more than I thought I could, and that I didn't need him to do it. I hopped faster, determined not to let him win.

"Ha! Like you could ever beat me!" I shouted across the short distance between us.

My legs pushed harder and harder against the ground, straining to make each hop larger than the last. The gap between us decreased steadily as I gained on him, and I felt like I was floating ten feet off the ground when I pulled up to his side, just a few feet from certain victory.

Out of the corner of my eye, I saw him redouble his efforts, closing the gap.

I hopped faster, determined to gain *all* the bragging rights. If I was going to look ridiculous in front of this many strangers, it was going to be for a good reason.

But just as I increased my speed, my left ankle turned under me, causing me to stumble into Lucas's side and pull him off balance. I cried out as the world spun and we both went careening toward the hard cement below, my worst fears realized.

I closed my eyes and braced for impact, but it never came. Or, at least, not as I had expected.

I hesitantly opened my eyes, breathing heavily, trying to make sense of what happened.

Lucas had somehow pulled me down on top of him so that he was the one who bore the brunt of the fall, and I was cushioned by his torso. His arms were wrapped around me, crushing me to him, his phone in his hand digging uncomfortably into my back as he clung to it. My own phone was pressed between us as my hands had awkwardly landed on his pectoral muscles, no doubt giving the Pixie Crew a lovely close-up of Lucas's chest.

His voice was frantic, breathless.

"Leah! Leah, are you ok? I'm so sorry. I'm so, so sorry."

Releasing his arms, his hands desperately framed my face even as his eyes searched mine, looking for the truth of my status. I could feel the guilt radiating off of him in waves.

I was stunned speechless. Being that close to Lucas, processing the crazy brave way he threw his body beneath mine to protect me, it was all so overwhelming.

"I ... yeah. I'm okay. It's okay. Really. Are you okay? Oh my gosh, I'm still on top of you. And you must be hurt. Oh no. Okay. Just let me ..."

I moved to slide off of him, but his arms only moved to a tighter, more comfortable position around my back, still holding me.

Something shifted in his eyes, suddenly taking on an intensity that I'd never seen in Lucas before.

I froze.

We had an audience, quite a large one, in fact, after all our antics, and I was aware of all the eyes on us. A Cast Member had called for backup when they saw us fall, and in the corner of my eye, I saw a paramedic jogging our way.

But all of the crowds and chaos around us faded away as I felt Lucas's fingertips move up the center of my spine.

I held my breath.

"I'm fine Leah." He gave a sly smirk. "But you won't be."

His touch had addled my brain, and in the fog of feeling things I shouldn't, I could only manage, "*Huh?*"

And that's when Lucas slowly released the arm holding me close and stretched it above his head, touching the cool metal of the entrance gate. I watched his hand move with utter confusion before realization hit me.

My mouth dropped open.

No way.

He cocked his head to the side beneath my own, which was hovering above him, inching his way closer to my face while smirking up at me. The peppermint-gum scent of his breath overwhelmed me as his eyes danced along with mine, the light in them unmistakable.

"You won't be fine, because I *win*."

Chapter 7

Lucas

I was standing in the queue for Mr. Toad but also for Snow White at the same time. Or at least it felt that way. Because my eyes were glued to Leah's live stream even while I waited for one of my favorite rides.

Eric nudged me from behind. "Hey Lucas, the line moved like five minutes ago."

I was startled out of my smitten stupor to see that there was an embarrassing amount of space between me and the mother and daughter in the matching pink Minnie ears ahead of me.

"What's got you smiling like that?" Eric asked with a grin, peeking over my shoulder to glance at my screen. He'd been busy gathering footage for his own content and hadn't really noticed my habit of dropping in on Leah's stream throughout the night. I was taking an evening off from live streaming because, for some reason, my head just hadn't been in the game today.

Who was I kidding? I knew *exactly* why my head wasn't in the game, and it had everything to do with the beautiful golden-haired goddess on my screen whose large emerald eyes I couldn't forget if I tried.

"*Ohhh*, I see. It all makes sense now." Eric laughed. "I didn't know you knew Leah."

"We met a few days ago. She's absolutely brilliant. You know her?"

"Yeah, she's good friends with Colette. You know. The one who …"

Eric looked around and, knowing ears were all around us, just gave me an eyebrow quirk that communicated what he couldn't say out loud.

Suddenly I remembered. Eric and Colette had a history, but it wasn't one he liked to talk about. They still hung out in the same circles once in a while, and from what he told me, it was always awkward. I wished I had advice for him, but I thought it kinder to just move past what he wasn't ready to face.

"Oh. Right. Colette. So … what do you know about Leah, then? If they are friends, and you and Colette are, uh, friends, that means you must know *something*."

Eric sighed. "Actually, dude, no, I don't know much. Colette told me that Leah's a really private person, and she doesn't share much about her life."

I gaped at him. That didn't sound like the Leah I met. The one who sat on the bench with me in Frontierland and handed over valuable pieces of herself to me—an absolute stranger. Leah, who stood next to me last night and quietly shared with me how the Disney castles made her feel protected and secure. The one who had let me hold her for a moment after we fell during that ridiculous park hopping dare, even though I was wholly undeserving of the privilege.

She was a private person? And yet, with me, she wasn't?

Interesting.

I tried not to get my hopes up as I cleared my throat and shook my head at the implications. No way. Not a chance. Right?

"Really?" I asked casually. "Like … ever? Huh."

Eric shook his head. "Nope. She knows a lot about Disney history though. Maybe even more than you do."

I laughed out loud. "I'm gathering that. If she truly does, I'll just have to marry her to keep her close."

I said it in jest, with a smile, but Eric could see more than most people.

He looked at me straight on and, with a knowing smirk, simply replied, "I bet you will."

Uncomfortable with the turn our conversation had taken—and how at home I was with that idea—I turned back to Leah's stream and watched as she explained about the scary trees in Snow White that were inspired by art director Gustaf Tenggren, and how his idea of terrifying trees reaching for you was then brought over to the Haunted Mansion by Claude Coats.

"She knows about the trees, Eric."

"I know, dude. I'm telling you, she's the real deal."

I looked up at the preview mural for Mr. Toad's Wild Ride as we entered Toad Hall, thinking about all the creators I'd met who thought they knew Disney History, but who really only knew what I liked to call the "popular" Disney history. The history everyone already knew, or rumors that had been passed around so often as truth that no one realized they weren't true at all.

But Leah? She knew about the trees. And Marc Davis's alternate Pirates ending for Walt Disney World. And John Hench's Snow White statue mistake. She knew it all and then some.

I slipped my phone into my pocket as Eric and I climbed into an Arrow Development-designed black car with red pinstriping and the name "Ratty" emblazoned on the front. While Eric drove like a madman on the way to nowhere in particular, I wondered why Leah was so guarded with her life but seemed so free and easy with me.

Maybe she trusted me. Maybe even liked me.

My heart did a little shimmy like the Blaine Gibson-sculpted devils at the thought as we drove through the very hot room at the end of the ride.

I had to see her.

But I didn't want to be obvious about it. I wasn't one for games, and usually I'd been pretty straightforward when I liked someone in the past, but more than ever before, I wanted to be careful about coming on too strong.

Because it was Leah.

My Leah.

Whoa.

Where did that come from?

I shook my head, mentally reeling in my enthusiasm. I didn't want to scare Leah away.

Eric gave me a quizzical look at my odd behavior before asking, "Where to next?"

I hesitated. I knew Leah had been in line for Snow White a few minutes ago. Was she off the ride yet? I looked around the courtyard, searching for the tell-tale blue dress she was wearing today in her beautiful Provincial Belle Disney bound. The one that made her eyes greener than the grass Belle spins around in, craving adventure in the great wide somewhere.

Not that I noticed or anything.

Eric was looking at his phone, and I realized he had pulled up Leah's live stream. Not only that, but she was walking right toward us.

My heart did its devilish wiggle again and skipped a beat at the sight of her, lovelier in person than on the screen of my phone.

As she drew near, she narrated to her live stream audience, "Look who I found! It's LucasDisNerd and EricOnTheHunt! Wave hi to your adoring fans, guys."

Her eyes caught mine, and my tongue suddenly felt tied up like the mouse's tail in *Cinderella*. While Eric waved hello, I gulped, gave myself a mental shake, and tried to think of something casual to say. But after an awkward ten seconds of just staring at the gorgeous creature before me, my true thoughts just fell out of my mouth.

"You look beautiful tonight, Leah."

She blushed and Eric offered up a small, discreet smile, chuckling under his breath.

He leaned in close to me and said quietly, "You're a goner, Lucas. I know when I'm not needed. You two have fun." He then made his excuses to Leah about some footage he needed to shoot elsewhere in the park before waving goodbye, leaving me and Leah in the center of Fantasyland, wondering what to do next.

Leah

My chat was flying ever since they caught a glimpse of Lucas.

KyloFanGirl100: *yay we get to hang with the two best Disney history nerds again!*

DisneeLuv23: *He's such a nice guy, I watched his live this morning & he was handing out personalized thank you notes to CMs*

MinnieMags: *I love to hear him talk *sigh**

User5696789: *He's hot. Instant follow.*

I couldn't argue with that, though I didn't love that someone else was saying it. Lucas was even more gorgeous than I remembered. Having him so near made those bread-and-butterflies dance again, and while I tried to collect myself by talking to everyone on my live about the origins of the 1922 carousel, the words kept coming out sideways and upside down. I flushed, angry with myself for sounding like a complete idiot.

Lucas had been studying my face intensely as I spoke, which only made my tied tongue worse. But then he did the unexpected.

"May I?" He gestured to my phone.

It took me a moment to register that he was asking about taking my live stream.

"Oh! Oh, yeah, of course. Be my guest."

I handed him my phone with the charger attached. It fit easily into the palm of his large hand. My fingers seemed to tingle where they had accidentally brushed against his during the handoff, and I quickly looked away so he couldn't see my face flush.

Lucas smiled at the screen and said his hellos before enthusiastically sharing about how the real carousel horses were solid wood while the replicas were fiberglass, and how you could tell if you were on a real one by tapping it. I stood in awe. His easy, unassuming charisma charmed my viewers as surely as it wove its spell around me.

My thoughts spun faster than the Astro Orbiter as I started to follow Lucas around Fantasyland, each of us pointing out facts to the other, lost in our little world of history and Imagineering.

We sauntered out through Frontierland and around the Rivers of America, heading toward the Haunted Mansion. I knew my wifi signal would never hold there, and thought it might be a good time for a break. But as I leaned closer to Lucas to mention this idea, an electric scooter came towards us, almost sideswiping me. Immediately, Lucas swung into action, his arm coming around me and pulling me to him and out of harm's way. The scooter's oblivious driver didn't even stop.

My breathing was erratic. My heart rate soared.

Not here.

Not again.

Why did my mind always go back to that place any time a vehicle swung a little too close?

Panic started to rise up and wrap its suffocating hand around my throat, even with Lucas's arm tight around me. He hadn't let go.

Lucas, thankfully, had also not let go of my phone in the incident. His laugh at someone's comment was half-hearted, as he tightened his hold on me. Through the fog of the panic attack I was trying to suppress, I heard him reassure people that I was okay, but that we were going to take a quick break. I could hear concern etched into every syllable. Most of my viewers didn't know I was emotionally drowning, and somehow he intuited that I needed to keep it that way.

Shame washed over me at falling apart in front of Lucas again for the second time, and it compounded my panic. He slipped my phone into his pocket as he maneuvered me around Fowler's Harbor to the quiet, hidden place behind the docked *Columbia Sailing Ship*.

The second we were out of sight of the crowds, Lucas embraced me, tucking me against himself as though I was always meant to be there. His chin rested on my head, and he ran his hand up and down my spine in a soothing motion.

Silent tears ran down my cheeks as I buried my face in his white vintage Mickey Mouse Club tee.

I gulped in air, and my whole body quaked, remembering.

Wanting to forget.

Needing to forget.

But the scenes rolled through my mind again and again, the ugly words beating me into a bloody pulp.

Lucas's hands stilled on my back. My panic grew. I was too much for him. This was too much. He didn't want or need to be my babysitter. He was done.

No.

Please.

Not when I had just started to feel comfortable and secure for the first time since—

Since.

In desperation, I slid my hands around his waist, leaning in and holding on.

It was all I could do, just to hold on.

Maybe he would stay just a moment longer if I held on.

But then, instead of pulling away, I heard him start to hum a tune I knew better than the twists of Big Thunder Mountain.

Stay Awake from Mary Poppins.

The song my mother used to sing to me before tucking me into bed every night. The movie I watched over and over for comfort when my parents died. The music that was woven into the tapestry of my life. And here he was, singing my very own song back to me.

As he gently rocked me, holding me close to his heart, every racing thought I had came to a complete stop.

I was safe.

I wasn't in control at this moment, but Lucas was.

And Lucas was safe. I don't know how I knew, but I just *knew*.

I turned my face up to find his blue eyes focused on me, laced with concern, and with something else I couldn't identify. A light breeze ruffled his hair and whispered an unspoken promise in this place where we found each other.

The sounds around us suddenly amplified. The laughter of those who had just splashed down the former Chickapin Hill. The cry of children whose day was over. The murmuring of a thousand tired but happy guests.

But all I cared about was the man right in front of me.

Something shifted in his eyes, and my breath caught at the sight. Suddenly the closeness of our embrace held more meaning than a friend comforting a friend. I found myself leaning in closer, tilting my head up. Lucas was going to kiss me. I could feel it.

Was I ready for that? I barely knew him. He barely knew me. This was crazy.

Colette's words of warning echoed in my head, that Lucas was a good guy who needed someone who could be honest with him. Open with him. My mind amplified them into a barrage of self-incrimination.

I wasn't good enough for Lucas.

He deserved better.

Clearly, he was just holding me out of pity because, for some reason, I couldn't seem to hold it together when I was around him. I was usually so strong, but something about him made me ... weak?

No.

Not weak.

Vulnerable. Open. Unhidden.

I let that truth pour over me, washing away the toxicity of my broken thoughts. Maybe I wasn't so damaged that I couldn't let someone in, even just a little bit.

Lucas has seen my "Mad Madam Mim" side, and he hadn't run. He'd chosen to stay. And now he wanted to kiss me.

Me.

I closed my eyes in anticipation.

Lucas

I swallowed in frustration as I watched Leah tilt up her chin and close her eyes. I hadn't meant to move to kiss her, and the last thing I wanted to do was take advantage of her in her vulnerable state.

But holding her near to my heart in this world of ours beside the inky waters of the Rivers of America, shifted something in me.

I suddenly felt purposeful. Strong. Needed. Desired.

Hers.

And it was that crazy thought that made my heart start to race. That made me move to do something that would be as easy as breathing with Leah.

The sound of a scooter beeping nearby brought me back to the reason we were hiding out behind a replica 1770s sailing ship. She didn't need me complicating whatever she was going through.

I kicked myself for getting this physically invested in the moment when Leah was clearly traumatized by something significant. I redirected my aim from her mouth, where I desperately wanted to land, and instead placed a gentle kiss on her forehead, lingering longer than I should as I mentally cataloged the scent of her peach shampoo.

Leah inhaled sharply. I wonder if even *that* was farther than I should have gone, but it was too late to take it back.

I pulled back from her, dropping her from my embrace to give her some space, in case her thoughts were at war as much as my own. Maybe she needed, like I did, a second to reconcile our new relational paradigm with the fact that we had only known each other a short while.

Then I caught the crestfallen look on her face and realized I had made a horrible mistake.

She looked devastated. Like she believed I didn't want to kiss her.

Like hell, I didn't.

But my resolve stood. She had been through enough tonight, and I didn't want to overwhelm her, even though everything in me ached to get closer to Leah.

I reached down and intertwined my hand with hers, letting the heat of our pressed-together palms communicate the truth of the feelings I couldn't express to her in other ways yet. She looked down at our hands and then quickly back up at me. Questioning. Hopeful.

I just gave her a grin and a wink before tugging her forward and declaring, "It's time to go pay our respects to the Ghost Host, I hear he's been dying to see us."

We moved as one toward the eerie lights of the Haunted Mansion, and the tinkling sound of Leah's laughter at my corny joke tucked itself all the way into my heart.

Chapter 8

Leah

I sang along with the beloved Peter Pan tune as I wove my way around the second star to the right and off to Neverland, perched above it all in my flying pirate galleon. Two months had passed since I'd met Lucas, and "flying" was an apt description of my current emotional state.

We had started to develop a routine, finding each other as soon as we arrived in the parks each day. We spent our time swapping Disney history stories and getting to know each other as well as we could while hundreds of strangers listened in.

Well, I got to know him, at least. I did my best to avoid any of his questions that had the potential to go where I couldn't let them. So I shared some about growing up in Northern California near the ocean, and how I used to throw rocks in the waves for fun when I was little. I kept my stories to the distant past, to tales that couldn't lead to what I desperately wanted to keep from Lucas.

I wished I could erase all of it from my mind forever, that night that changed my whole life.

As I flew over London, I aimed my phone toward the tiny ant-like cars moving along the streets.

"The original car traffic effect was achieved by painting a rotating bicycle chain with glow-in-the-dark paint." I rattled off facts to my online friends, digging into the history and the details. I had to, in order to distract myself from the awful truth. From the bile that threatened to rise up every time I saw a moving vehicle, even fake miniature ones.

All of it reminded me that I was just as guilty as Max was, that I had let him get away with stealing away her life and mine, all at the same time.

As if I had summoned him, Max showed up in the chat.

User78398642: *I CAN SEE YOU.*

User78398642: *I'M COMING TO FIND YOU*

User78398642: *SEE YOU SOON, LEAH BIRD*

As I sailed over a miniature Neverland glowing in UV light, I stuttered mid-sentence. My moderator besties instantly jumped on, deleting and blocking the threats, but the damage had already been done.

My body had gone into fight or flight. In between shallow breaths, I peered over the edge of my pirate galleon. I wished I could jump out and lose myself in the land where mermaids, lost boys, and fairies reigned. Instead, I closed my eyes and refused to be sick.

He couldn't get to me. I knew that. I had made sure of it. He was just trying to scare me.

It was working.

I forced myself to open my eyes again. Pixie dust fell on Peter Pan and Wendy as I realized I'd been silent on my live stream for most of the ride. I refocused back to my chat, only to find my friends taking care of me as usual.

MinnieMags: *Are you ok Leah?*

CastlEvie: *Leah, it's ok if you need to take a break. We'll be here when you get back.*

I took a deep, shuddering breath. They knew me so well; they had witnessed over and over again how much these comments got to me.

"Yeah, um, sorry guys, I do need to take a quick breather. Thank you for having my back as always. I appreciate it so much."

I waved goodbye and ended my live, exiting Peter Pan and merging into the Fantasyland crowds. I squinted in the bright sun, my eyes instinctively darting around, searching faces, seeing Max everywhere and nowhere as my thoughts collided with each other.

I headed for the one place that would ground me, my favorite spot in the whole park, coaching myself into calm the whole way.

Just through the tunnel.

Almost there.

Breathe.

And finally, I was there, standing in front of Snow White, listening to her song echoing in the wishing well and letting the sounds of the waterfall wash over me. I focused on the rotating fish in the water, letting each spin soothe my anxious thoughts with its repetitive motion.

"Leah!"

My head flew up in a panic, all sense of peace instantly slithering away. But it wasn't Max advancing toward me over the bridge. It was Lucas, making his way to me with a furrowed brow and a look of deep concern etched on his face.

Suddenly, it was like he'd caught my escaping peace and returned it back to me. He wrapped his arms around my shaking frame in a fierce embrace. My arms felt like those of a pre-programmed audio-animatronic as they flew around him, too.

I buried my face in his shoulder and breathed deeply, feeling a kind of safety I'd never imagined would be possible again. He didn't say anything, just held me there as strollers and curious onlookers passed us, his head gently resting on my own, rocking us back and forth.

As Lucas held me, one thing became clear: I didn't know what my future looked like, or how to escape my past, but in that moment, I knew that I didn't want him to *ever* let me go.

Lucas

As I held Leah, my blood boiled beneath the surface.

I had been watching her live, finishing a fried chicken lunch at the Plaza Inn, a throwback to the Swift Chicken Plantation chicken dinners that cost only $1.50 in 1955. But then dark threats poured into her chat. I lost my appetite as soon as I saw them. Throwing the rest of my meal away, I hurried toward Fantasyland where I had hoped to find Leah.

And she was there, right where I thought she would be, at the fountain.

It was instinct that made me reach for her and fold her into my arms. I wanted to protect her. I wanted to close her off from the cruel world that seemed to sever her joy at every turn.

She needed a safe place to fall apart, and I was determined to be that place for her.

A security guard friend of mine walked by, clearly keeping an eye on our situation. He gave me a cocked eyebrow and a raised chin, inquiring about Leah. I nodded slightly and mouthed, "*She's okay*." Ed gave me a small nod in return and continued on, passing by to give us privacy but not leaving the area completely.

I laid my head on top of Leah's, taking deep breaths to help calm her even as a sense of danger and dread threatened to creep into the edges of our peaceful moment. Whoever was sending her those messages had to stop.

I would find a way to make them stop. I *had* to.

For Leah.

As if she heard me say her name in my mind, she raised her head at that moment, meeting my eyes.

"You saw it, didn't you."

It wasn't really a question, but I answered anyway.

"Yeah. I saw it. Leah, please tell me what's going on. Let me help."

Leah sighed and took a step back, out of my arms. I instantly felt the loss.

"You can't help, Lucas. It's ... complicated."

"I am okay with complicated. Leah, you have someone who is clearly deranged harassing you and sending threats. Now is not the time to be mysterious or vague. I need details so I can help you. And by God, I *will* find a way to keep you safe. You aren't alone in dealing with this. I'm here. Trust me. Let me help."

Leah looked at her feet for a moment, clearly contemplating my words. The happy melody of "Fortuosity" from *The Happiest Millionaire* drifted by us from the castle hub as she wrung her hands together, wrestling internally. I wished I knew what was in her head, why she constantly shut me out and would only give me glimpses of her life here and there.

Finally, after a wait that felt longer than standby for Rise of the Resistance, she raised her head and spoke, slowly and quietly.

"Lucas, I do trust you. So much. More than anyone, really. And I do want your help. But I need some time to sort out what I can share without it being ... without you getting ... without him..." she broke off. "I just need some time. Please?"

Frustrated, I blew out a breath I didn't realize I'd been holding. I looked beyond her to the castle that held as many dreams as I held for whatever this was between me and Leah. I knew I couldn't push. That Leah, for whatever reason, knew she wasn't ready, and I wanted to respect that.

But in that moment, I needed her to understand. To see me. To know.

"Fine. I will be on standby for when you are ready. But Leah?"

"Yeah?"

"Come with me." I extended my hand.

She smiled. "Why? Where are we going?"

"You'll see."

Leah bit her bottom lip and cautiously slipped her hand into mine.

I entwined our fingers and heard her gasp at the surprise of it, as I pulled her confidently along behind me. I buzzed with joy and nerves as I led her up the stairs tucked to the left of the fountain, the trees hiding us away from the bustling world.

"Oh, I already know about the Peter Pan & Wendy Darling's initials on the tree, but did you know—oh!"

Leah's words were cut off as I pulled her abruptly to a stop, my free arm coming around her back to gather her close to me, still keeping her hand intertwined with my own. I leaned my forehead against hers as I whispered words I wanted only her to hear. Words that I was terrified would make her run, but I had to risk it.

"Leah, you are the most exquisite being I have ever known. Somehow, in just a few months, you have become the wonderful thought that I wake to each day, and fall asleep to each night. Leah ... I want to kiss you."

Leah was quiet.

I closed my eyes, afraid of the very real possibility that I just permanently ruined our friendship. That she didn't feel what I felt. That, in that brilliant, beautiful mind of hers, she was busy formulating a way to let me down gently.

But then I felt her lips touch mine. Gingerly at first, and then, as she gathered confidence, she dropped my hand, wound her arms around my neck, and dove into the kiss in earnest. Leah shifted her weight against me, connecting us more firmly, and, as elation replaced shock, I deepened the kiss, my heart soaring like it had been sprinkled with pixie dust.

It was more than I could have hoped for. More than I'd imagined. My Princess Leah chose to kiss me in the shadow of the castle at the happiest place on Earth.

As our connection naturally slowed, I pulled back to find Leah's eyes. I was so desperate to see her, this woman who had irrevocably changed my world but didn't even know it yet.

Leah's eyes shined as she looked up at me, offering just a few simple words that were all I ever needed to hear.

"You're my happy thought, too."

Chapter 9

Leah

As the final notes died down from the exit music of *Fantasmic Reimagined,* I ended my live stream with all my online friends, wishing them a magical evening and a great, big, beautiful tomorrow. I looked over at Lucas, who had launched into the history of *Fantasmic!* and the renovations to the areas around the Rivers of America to accommodate how the show had grown over the years.

"Don't forget to tell them about the Jean Lafitte anchor!" I interjected as I popped over his shoulder, waving to all our mutual friends. "I'm going to go grab a Mickey bar, do you want anything, Lucas?"

"Could you grab me some popcorn? I'll send you the money after I hop off the live."

I waved him away. "No need. One Walt special coming right up. If only you had some freshly squeezed orange juice to go with it!" I joked, laughing as I walked off to complete my task.

My heart felt lighter than it had in years. I practically skipped my way to the popcorn stand, thinking about how I used to dress up as Cinderella when I was little. I would run down the wooden stairs in our two-story home, properly attired in my blue and white sparkly dress, purposefully forgetting my shoe along the way. Outside, my best friend Bianca would be ready and waiting as coachman, tying my red wagon to the back of her bike with some purple yarn from my mother's stash of odds and ends. I would hop in and she would pedal furiously toward her playhouse, a pink one with brown shutters and quaint flower boxes that her dad had made for her.

It all felt so long ago. When I looked in the mirror now, all I saw looking back at me was a shadow of who I once was, almost unrecognizable except for the Mickey ears on my head and the green eyes that had looked back at me my whole life.

But that sweet, innocent little girl was still in there somewhere. That, I believed. More and more, I was watching her come back to life. Every firework show that left me in tears, every spin of the teacups, each time I gave Mickey a hug or ate a churro by the castle—it was all so very *healing*. It gave me hope that I could reclaim the part of me that was lost.

The part Max had stolen.

And he had stolen it. That, at least, I could admit now. I squared my shoulders as I finished paying and accepted the brightly colored box of popcorn from the cast member. I gave them a smile and said thank you before heading to the ice cream cart for my Mickey bar.

Being with Lucas was like raising the theatrical scrim that had been obscuring the way I thought about Max. Much like how the endless hallway of the Haunted Mansion uses illusion to hide the mechanism making the floating candelabra move, so too had Max's devotion been all smoke and mirrors.

He used me. He blamed me for anything that went wrong in our relationship. And he knew exactly how to hold me captive, twisting my love and affection for him into something he could manipulate to get what he wanted.

As I waited in line, I checked my latest social media posts for comments, trying to get my mind off of Max. I attempted to keep up with posted comments as much as I could. Everyone deserved to be seen and heard, but some days were easier than others. As I scrolled the comments section, joking around with some people and answering the park questions of others, I ran into one that made my blood run cold.

I KNOW WHAT YOU DID. I WILL FIND YOU.

Frozen with a fear I should have been used to already, I took a deep breath and closed my eyes, repeating the phrases that got me through each day.

You are safe here.

He can't get to you.

You are in control now.

I reported and blocked Max yet again, one of the thousands of fake accounts he had made just to get to me. But the damage had been done. He'd gotten what he wanted. Max fed off my fear, and he knew just how to get to me.

I'd lost my appetite.

It felt like I'd lost so much more.

Memories started creeping into my happy place like the hitchhiking ghosts following me home. Like the time Max called me a horrible name for accidentally making eye contact with a handsome stranger in a cafe before dragging me out to the car and making me feel less than human for my lapse in attention.

Or when he had stolen my phone and deleted some of the pictures because, as he put it, I "looked too fat that day" or "wasn't wearing suitable clothing." Max also removed all pictures of me with former guy friends, even if we had just been hanging out and had no romantic attachment. He claimed it was "to protect his little bird's reputation" because what would people think of me if they saw me with all those men?

And then there was that one time when he got angry and shoved me into a display of glass ornaments inside the crystal shop in New Orleans Square, claiming that I had ignored him when I had simply stopped to talk to some friends.

He got banned from Disneyland that day. I got 14 stitches.

It was all red flags. All of it. And I knew, deep down, that it wasn't ok, because it just felt ... off. But the apologies and excuses he painted across my doubt were laced with words of love, protection, and flattery, to the point where I was convinced he was only doing all those things for my own good because that's what people did when they loved you. Or so I thought at the time.

I ditched the Mickey bar line with a huff of frustration. Why had I let Max get to me again? I carried the popcorn back to Lucas, finding him on his makeshift seat on the gray stone ledge lining the tiered esplanade before the Rivers of America. He was still on his live, showing people the ducklings who skittered below him, nibbling on bits of old popcorn as they dutifully followed their mama.

Quietly taking a seat next to him, I put the popcorn between us. His head was practically between his knees as he contorted himself for the perfect shot of the five fuzzy ducklings. The ridiculous image of him stole into my heart. It was like magic, the way seeing him could make the corners of my mouth pull up.

Straightening again, Lucas raised his head, laughing at the antics of the ducklings, but he paused when his eyes met mine.

He could see the truth of what had just happened on my face. I knew it as soon as his eyes grew stormy, his expression shifting into one of concern and fierce protectiveness.

But just as quickly, Lucas turned back to his live, rearranging his expression into one of easy nonchalance.

"Hey guys, I need to hop off for a minute. We'll go slide down the icy slopes of Matterhorn Mountain soon, I promise. See you in a few." Lucas hit the button to end the live, and then turned off his phone and slid it into his pocket.

I sent him a grateful look, but internally I was fighting the intense guilt that I felt for interrupting his work yet again with my inexplicable drama.

"Leah, what's going on? Are you okay?"

I looked down, not sure how much to share. If I was honest, I wanted to tell him everything. I was tired of holding on to the secrets, of sharing half-truths and avoiding specific topics.

I felt like the Pepper's Ghost dancers in the haunted ballroom. I was there but not, all at the same time. Lucas deserved so much more than that. He deserved someone who wasn't an illusion.

What part of me was actually real anymore?

Lucas waited patiently beside me, his hands clasped and his elbows resting on his knees. I was becoming completely lost in my own thoughts, but he never pushed me or grew irritated as I tried to find my words. He just kept his steady gaze on me, silently communicating that he was there, whenever I was ready.

Finally, I collected my thoughts enough that I could speak.

"It happened again. A threatening comment. But I dealt with it. Honestly, it's okay. Really."

His eyes held mine for a long time, silently questioning. I knew he wanted to help, and all the words he wanted to say, but he didn't speak them. Instead, he turned and picked up his popcorn box and extended it toward me.

"Want some?"

I breathed a sigh of relief. He understood. He didn't like it, but Lucas was, in his own way, communicating that he understood that I had to tell him on my own terms, in my own time. I grabbed a few kernels, and then he pulled the box back to claim some for himself. We sat in strained silence, sharing the salty snack while looking out at the sparkling water. The Rivers of America winked at us just beyond a stream of people headed either to Critter Country or Frontierland.

"Okay," said Lucas, "serious question."

My heart stopped. This was it. He was going to ask, and I was going to have to choose whether to lie or tell him everything. I knew this was coming ... it was unavoidable really. He needed to know.

I braced myself.

"What is your absolute FAVORITE moment of Fantasmic Reimagined?"

My breath left my body as laughter tumbled out of me.

Lucas grinned at me. He'd known I would react that way.

"Well ... it's pretty hard to beat when Tinker Bell swings over the crowd and sprinkles us with pixie dust. I always feel like I could fly at that moment. But ..."

I hesitated. I was afraid to give it the freedom to pass my lips, worried that Lucas would think it was silly. Max had always dismissed my "fairy tale" dreams as stupid and naive.

"What? It's not Tinker Bell?"

I shook my head.

"Then what?" Lucas nudged me playfully with his shoulder. "Come on, you can tell me."

I took a deep breath before speaking.

"You know when Rapunzel is looking up at all the floating lanterns, and Flynn Rider gently takes her hand and pulls her close, and then they dance and he sings to her? I love that moment. And their whole story, really. Rapunzel, for the way she finds her freedom with Flynn's help, and Flynn for the way loving Rapunzel changes his heart and purpose. They complement each other so beautifully. It's a fairy tale, but it's how love is supposed to look. How it's ... how it's never looked for me."

I blushed and looked down, embarrassed by how I had gotten so carried away with my explanation.

Lucas wasn't shy, though. His voice dropped to a quiet rumble as he leaned in closer. He asked, "Do you mean to tell me, my darling Leah, that no one's ever asked you to dance?"

My heart thundered like the railroad in the distance.

Could he hear it?

"I ... well ... not really, no."

"Never?"

I finally lifted my head to meet his gaze.

"No. No one ..." I bit my lip, unused to such unfiltered honesty, but soldiered on. "No one has ever asked me."

Lucas looked at me oddly for a moment before a smile slowly crept across his face. He set his popcorn box down on the stone wall between us, a few kernels falling to the ground, my heart tumbling after. Then he stood, his gaze holding mine before he swept back a step and stood before me. I followed his movements, my eyes growing large as I realized what he was about to do.

I started to panic, and a flood of words left my mouth before I could stop them.

"But I really never wanted to anyway. I didn't mean that you ... that we ..."

Lucas simply lifted a brow, cocked his head, and put on a knowing grin as he slowly held out an upturned hand, tucking his other behind his back in a gallant posture.

"Will you dance with me, Princess Leah?"

All of the breath left my body at once.

The *Mark Twain* slipped past on the moon-gilded water, puffing steam and churning dependably along as it did every fourteen minutes. Before us, a crowd swirled by, endless colors of excited and exhausted tourists, a sea of humanity that didn't realize that time had stopped next to the Rivers of America.

I closed my eyes and sucked in a breath. It was too much to process. Lucas didn't know what he was asking.

The last time I let someone get close, disaster followed.

What if I brought that into Lucas's life?

"Leah."

I exhaled all the air that had taken residence in my lungs. The way he said my name. Soft. Pleading. With that unmistakable inflection that told me, even with my eyes closed, that he was smiling

Maybe.

Maybe I *could*.

Maybe I could reach out and hold onto this moment of happiness, just once.

I opened my eyes to find his own blue ones pleading with me, his hand still outstretched. And before I knew what it was doing, my hand slid into his, allowing him to pull me to a stand.

My anxiety continued to ratchet up. "I don't know how to do this," I whispered, my voice shaking more than my hands.

Lucas just grinned down at me before pulling me in close and gathering my body to his own.

"Don't worry princess, I got you."

And, despite my best efforts, he absolutely did.

Lucas

Adrenaline pumped through my veins as I stepped in front of Leah, giving her my very best Prince Charming impression. I swallowed down my doubt, took a steadying breath, and offered her my hand.

I watched her face carefully.

I could read Leah like a book, and she had become the story I never wanted to stop reading. Every day she surprised me with her quick wit, her brilliant mind, and a passionate heart that showed itself when no one was looking. Right now, as she sat on the narrow stone wall next to my abandoned popcorn with her eyes tightly closed, I could tell she was wrestling with herself. Leah was serious. Leah was focused. Leah didn't dance.

But she could dance. She only had to choose it.

To choose me.

My heart clenched at the thought that she might not. But then as I observed her shaking her head and mumbling to herself, I found myself captivated by the simple delight of who she was. And I had an overwhelming desire to remind her that I was there for her, and that her secret wish to dance with someone was not silly in the least.

So I spoke her name, pouring every ounce of emotion I had into it.

Leah's response was like sunshine coming out from behind the clouds. Her eyes opened and met mine, and a brighter moment in my life I had not yet known. It was like every nighttime spectacular I'd ever witnessed rolled into one moment.

When her small hand found mine, I knew that I would never be the same. I could never be just Lucas Barsotti, digital creator and Disney history nerd.

No. Now, as I pulled Leah into my arms, I was more. I was Lucas, the one who had finally found his buried treasure.

I gathered Leah close, pulling her arm around my neck as my own wrapped around her waist. Her eyes peered up at me from under lashes that couldn't hide the unmistakable shine of unshed tears.

"What do we do now?" she asked, practically in a whisper.

"Now, we dance."

I waited for the downbeat before smoothly guiding her in a slow box step, using my arms to gently lead her where she needed to go. And, thankfully, she moved on hesitant but graceful feet.

At that moment, I had never been more thankful for all those times my mom insisted I needed to know the basics of ballroom dance. I remember rolling my eyes every time she said, "You'll thank me someday," while leading me around the living room to old records from the '40s cranking out rusty tunes on an ancient record player.

I made a mental note to call my mom and thank her later.

Leah pulled my attention back to the moment as her steps faltered, becoming suddenly stilted. Her eyes darted to the sides, looking wild and nervous.

"People are starting to stare, Lucas. Maybe this wasn't a good idea."

"Princess, this is the best idea I've ever had. Let them stare. This dance is just for you and me."

With that, I pulled her in, closer to my heart, brushing my lips against the strands of hair covering the shell of her ear. I needed her to stay in this moment with me, if only for a minute longer.

So I started to sing, soft words about seeing the light and how my world had shifted.

Leah let out a contented sigh and relaxed her cheek against my chest, our dance slowly morphing into a gentle sway as we lost and found all we needed in the magical bubble we'd made for ourselves. Onlookers be damned.

This was ours.

This place, this dance, this river, this park.

It was only ours, always.

Our very own happily ever after.

Chapter 10

Lucas

It felt like my feet hadn't touched the asphalt once since my dance with Leah. She was holding my hand as we stood together in line for the Matterhorn, our other hands busy holding our phones as we chatted with our online communities. But every so often, I would gently run my thumb over Leah's, feeling the warmth and softness of her skin, giving her a reminder that she was my priority and that my thoughts hadn't left her.

Her smile could have illuminated a thousand Main Streets as she explained about the hidden basketball half-court inside the mountain before us, used as a break room for cast members once upon a time. Her enthusiasm was contagious, and I threw in what I knew about it being the world's first tubular track coaster and how there used to be mountain climbers that would scale the peak.

When we reached the front of the line, Leah indicated to the cast member that we were a party of two, and we were placed in the back of the coaster, positions five and six. As we were waiting to load, I leaned in close to Leah over the gate separating us and whispered in her ear, "I wish they still had tandem ride vehicles for this like they used to."

As I pulled back, Leah gave me a confused look.

"Really? Why?"

I moved back to her, closer this time, my lips just brushing her ear. "So I could kiss you as much as I wanted."

Her blush was my reward as I gave her a bold wink before stepping forward through the open gate into the sadly-not-tandem bobsled.

We tugged on our yellow straps and before we knew it, we were clutching our phones for dear life as hearts flew on our screens and shouts of joy echoed through the ice caverns. Leah screamed each time the Yeti appeared, and I pointed out the old bobsled and skyway bucket embedded in the ice and snow.

As we crashed through the water at the end of the ride, I talked about the early construction phase, where Walt Disney insisted on trying out the Matterhorn's track before the brakes were finished. Their solution to keep him safe was to add loose bales of hay at the bottom of the run to slow the bobsleds down, which resulted in the hay being tossed into the air. Walt then insisted that this feeling of "flying into the hay" had to be included in the attraction, which was how the splashdown came to be, with water becoming a more practical hay-substitute.

After finishing my story, I caught Leah's gaze, her head angled over her shoulder as she looked back at me, grinning because we both knew what was coming. In unison, we recited the familiar safety spiel reminding us to remain seated, please.

My whole being felt lighter than Walt flying into the hay.

Glancing back at the chat, I noticed that my moderator friend Mia had been trying to get my attention while I was busy trying not to donate my phone to the Yeti by accident.

MsPixiedst: LUUUUCAAAAAS! Red alert! You need to see ParkGossip's latest post!!!

Everyone else was chiming in with the same message, and dread seeped into my bones. ParkGossip was notorious for fake news and for exaggerating stories, and they loved finding dirt on Disney creators and taking it to the extreme.

As I held out a hand to Leah to help her out of her bobsled, I tried to calm my racing heart and remind myself that I didn't have skeletons in my closet. I wasn't hiding anything.

Leah took my hand, but when her eyes met mine, my sense of unease only increased.

All the color had drained from her face, and it was clear by her choppy, short breathing that she was going into a full-blown panic attack.

Clearly, she had received the same message I had.

I pulled her through the exit gate and out onto the pier where the Motor Boat Cruise used to launch once upon a time. It was nearly empty, all of the crowds gathering closer to Small World for a better view of the second nighttime parade. We found a pair of chairs at a table near the end, and I paused my live so that I could give Leah my full attention. She had never looked so terrified since I'd known her.

"*Breathe*, Leah, I need you to breathe."

Leah shook her head, grasping her phone and desperately punching in the search for ParkGossip. She must have ended her live while she waited in the unloading area.

"I have to know. *Now*."

And when the video popped up, Leah gasped. Because there, for all the world to see, was a video of us dancing together in New Orleans Square.

I saw red. How could they post such a private moment? We hadn't told our followers we were together yet; they just knew we were friends. I was waiting for Leah's lead as to when and how to tell everyone. And we were going to, soon. We'd talked about it a few times. It just felt so new to us, and with so much of our world public all the time, it felt too special to share with the world yet.

But there it was. That choice had been stolen from us. It didn't get more public than that.

People had already tagged us both repeatedly in the comments of the video, and some other creators had made duet videos cheering us on, which did take the sting out of it a bit. I smiled, seeing one of my best creator friends HenryAroundtheWorld outside the Walt Disney World wedding pavilion pretending to get ready for a wedding with me and Leah tagged.

"Leah, I know this is not what we wanted, but it's not that bad. We were going to tell people eventually, right?"

Leah was quiet, disturbingly so. Her eyes were fixed on the screen in front of her, the video on repeat in an endless loop.

Then she spoke.

"Lucas, you have to know … that dance with you, that was the best moment of my life."

Her voice broke on the last word, and she paused to gather herself before continuing.

"Please don't ever think I'm ashamed of you or didn't want people to know about us being together. It's not that."

I took in her words, weighing them in my mind for a moment before responding.

"I never thought you would be. But I am worried about you. What's going on, Leah?"

My voice cracked with the depth of my emotion, and I cleared my throat before continuing.

"I can't keep you safe if you won't tell me what's wrong. And I've never cared for someone in my entire life as much as I care about you. I want you more than I want the People Mover back."

I gave a small smile, then took a deep breath before continuing. "You've quickly become everything to me. Everything. Tell me how I can help. *Please*, Leah."

"You don't understand!" Leah abruptly stood and started pacing, frustration pouring off her.

She spun toward me, words violently spilling out of her pretty mouth—words that didn't make any sense.

"I was trying to keep *you* safe. *You*, Lucas. And now he knows about you. And I've done exactly what I was trying not to do. I've ruined you as much as I've ruined me, all because I thought I could live out some stupid fantasy and maybe actually fall in love with an absolutely perfect guy who is more than everything I ever could have imagined or deserved."

I felt like I'd gone over Schweitzer Falls. I didn't understand most of what Leah was throwing in my direction, but I did hear the word love.

Love.

Did Leah love me?

Because I sure-as-small-world loved her. Her chaos, her heart for her community, her subtle humor, her excitement about the nerdiest, tiniest park details ... she was my match. My soulmate.

My love.

Leah was still talking, but I didn't hear a word she said. I stepped in close, slowly lifting up my arms and skimming my hands along the perfect contours of her face, framing it in my palms and brushing my thumbs over her soft skin.

She was startled into silence by my sudden closeness, and at that moment, her eyes became my new home. They shimmered more than the water that surrounded us on three sides, and I knew then that I had to tell her. She had to know.

Still cradling her face in my hands, I spoke softly.

"I've waited my whole life for you, Leah. Every time I stood in front of the castle, every coin I tossed in the wishing well, every time I walked down Main Street at the end of the night, I have only ever been wishing for you. I love you more than I thought I could ever love another human being. And someday soon, I hope to stand in all those places with you, holding hands and looking into our future together as man and wife. But for now, all I need from you is to know that I can help keep you safe. Because while Disney will always be my land, you are now my *entire* world."

And before Leah could reply, I brought my lips to hers in a kiss that poured out every ounce of emotion that I felt for her. She instantly responded, giving a little cry as she deepened our connection, returning my fervor with abandon. The world around us faded away as we met, again and again, tasting and loving and kissing, standing like the pier below us on the edge of what used to be and what was now.

Leah pulled back, the tears she had tried so hard to hold back now streaming down her face.

"Lucas, I love you, too. So much. You are like the piece of me I didn't know was missing. You believe in me more than I believe in myself. You've allowed me to feel freer than I've ever been."

Elated, I moved in to claim her mouth for another kiss. But Leah put her hands on my chest and held me back, looking into my eyes to make sure I heard the next words she spoke.

"But before you decide to make me your entire world, I need to tell you who I *really* am."

Leah

I could see confusion and concern warring in his eyes, and I winced internally. This was not how I wanted to tell him. If I ever wanted to tell him.

I looked away from him and watched a duck bob under the dark water beside us, casting ripples out toward the shore. How I wished my life didn't do the same to everyone around me.

But he had to know. Now. For his own safety.

I took a deep breath.

"Two years ago, I dated a guy named Max." I felt Lucas tense up next to me, but I pushed forward. "He was not ... like you. He was jealous and controlling, and sometimes he ...

well, he …" I let my eyes drift back to the duck, now paddling away from us toward Small World.

"He *what*, Leah?"

I closed my eyes and swallowed, my mouth suddenly as dry as a trip on the Mine Train through Nature's Wonderland in July.

"He … let his anger show in more ways than just words."

Lucas muttered a curse before pulling me in for a fierce hug. I let him hold me, the sobs bubbling up again. But I choked them back, knowing what needed to happen, and hating that it did. He deserved to have all of the truth I had withheld, if only to understand what I needed to do and why.

"There's more. One night, he caught me looking at an online profile of an old friend from high school because I wanted to see a picture of his new baby. I wasn't even going to contact him or anything. But Max threw my phone across the room and shattered it. He called me … some names. Then he told me to get in the car, that we were going out. Knowing how he got when he drove angry, I suggested we should maybe stay home, so that we could relax a bit, trying to get him to calm down without telling him to calm down because he hated that. He didn't listen and threatened to hurt me if I didn't get in the car. So I grabbed my purse and slid into the passenger seat for the worst ride of my life."

"It wasn't long before we were weaving along the coast well above the speed limit, and I just kept clutching the handle of the door and trying to find ways to suggest we slow down, but I knew that anything I said would only make his pedal foot get closer to the floor. Suddenly he took a U-turn too fast and …"

Lucas looked at me with wide eyes and mouth agape. "Leah, please tell me you didn't drive off a cliff? How did you survive?"

Tears flowed down my cheeks as I shook my head. "No, we didn't fall off. But … there was a runner on the side of the road nearest the ocean and …" I couldn't finish. It was too horrible. My whole body started shaking, and I desperately tried to hide my face from the horror that had no doubt registered on Lucas's.

"Oh, *Leah*."

Those two words just made me cry harder. I'd never been so grateful for the sounds of the late-night parade, which drowned out each uncontrolled sob. But then I pulled back to look at his face and found ... pity. Concern. Not horror and disgust as I had expected.

"Don't you see?" I looked around, lowering my voice, ever mindful of who might be listening. "We *killed* someone, Lucas! Max only stopped to look over the edge for a moment, and when he realized the runner was long gone, swallowed up by the sea, he turned to me and said, 'You did this. You made me angry. That person would still be alive if you weren't so stupid. And if you ever breathe a word about this to anyone, I will tell them you were the one driving. It will be my word against yours. It was all your fault, after all.'"

Lucas's jaw tightened.

"No, Leah, NO. No, that wasn't your fault. How could it be? You were a victim of his abuse, forced into a dangerous situation, and then simply an observer of his poor choices that led to someone's death."

He paused for a moment, looking back at the Matterhorn behind us, lost in thought.

"Leah. Please tell me you went to the police despite what he said."

I looked down at my feet, feeling the beat of the music nearby vibrate through my chest. Shame washed over me like a poisonous wave, the same one that I drowned in every day when fear wasn't running the show.

"I ... I couldn't, Lucas. I was terrified. It was all I could do to get away and hide from Max. It took me almost a month to figure out how to get free. My aunt has an inn nearby, and there is a hidden apartment behind the lobby that Max doesn't know about. I hadn't talked to her in years, but as soon as I got a burner phone and reached out to her about needing a safe place, she didn't hesitate. She told me to come and stay with her as long as

I needed. And that's where I've been ever since, only taking a few steps between Disney property and the inn. And nowhere else. Because it's not safe. He knows what I know. And he wants me back. He wants me silent."

An uncomfortable silence settled over us. I inhaled a ragged breath, wishing our perfect world hadn't just imploded.

"Leah, this is a lot to take in."

My heart stopped beating. This was it. He saw who I really was, the unlovable truth about me. He was no doubt going to run away from me, and I didn't blame him.

"I know. I'm sorry Lucas," I whispered softly.

I gathered my courage and took a deep breath so I could get out my next words. Words I didn't want to say, but that I had to. There was no choice.

"I know this changes things. And I understand. Believe me. I don't fault you for wanting out. I wouldn't want me either, knowing all of this. So thank you. Thank you for your friendship, your humor, your love." Lucas's hand found mine, giving it a gentle squeeze. I swallowed. "You've restored pieces of me that I thought were lost." I paused, a sad smile forming. "As lost as the bats in the attic of the Haunted Mansion, Lucas. I've loved every second of every moment I've had with you, and I will never regret anything—except for what I had to keep from you so that you'd be safe. Safe from Max. Safe from being involved in a crime you had nothing to do with. And safe from getting hurt by the broken shards of my messed-up life."

"Leah, I—"

"No, Lucas, let me finish." He seamed his lips and nodded for me to continue. I took a deep breath, not sure I was ready to say what needed to be said.

"I love who you are and who you allowed me to be." I swallowed, dreading what came next. Closing my eyes, I let my final words flow out in a rush. "I hope someday you find someone who deserves you."

I turned around and fled before he could say any of his predictable placating words because I couldn't bear to hear a single one. I was practically running through the crowds, away from the heartache, away from the pain that I caused by loving someone I didn't deserve to love. Tears blurred my eyes, turning everyone into colorful blobs that I bobbed and weaved around as I stumbled away from the best man I'd ever known.

I made it as far as the submarines before I felt a hand on my arm pulling me backward.

Shock rippled through my body. I couldn't believe that he would come after me following all of that. A twinge of joy mixed with unworthiness swirled around me as I sobbed my relief out loud.

But when I spun around to try to reiterate to Lucas why I couldn't be with him, it wasn't his blue eyes that met mine.

No, these eyes were dark. Dangerous. Hostile.

Max.

Chapter 11

Lucas

I watched her go, dumbstruck. My brain kept screaming at me to move my feet, to chase after my Princess Leah, that none of what she said changed anything. But I couldn't fully take in what had just happened. Had she just broken up with me? Written me off as if I didn't understand that her ex was a violent monster who was trying to pin a murder on her?

Whose life was this?

I had never imagined I'd be holding my dream in my arms in one moment and be so completely alone in the next. I couldn't process any of this.

But processing could wait. I needed to go after Leah. *Now*.

Shaking off my shock, I strode in the direction she had taken, pulling my phone out to call her at the same time.

It went to voicemail.

Frustrated, I shoved my phone back into my pocket. Of course, she was so upset she'd turned her phone off. I went to all her favorite places in the park, searching for my Leah. The benches behind the Matterhorn. The Snow White fountain where we'd first met. The docks behind Fowler's Harbour. The waterfall tucked behind Winnie the Pooh.

Nowhere. She had to have left the park.

I muttered a curse, angry at myself for how I could have been so incredibly stupid and slow to react. I didn't even know where she lived, which made so much more sense now. I had always known she was a private person, but I could never have guessed the real reason why.

I pulled out my phone and texted the only people I could trust: Eric and Henry.

Me: I need help. I lost Leah.

Eric: What? What do you mean you lost her?

Henry: Yeah, we're gonna need more context, bro

I took a deep breath, the reality of my situation causing my hands to shake as I fumbled with the right words to explain without betraying Leah's trust.

Me: She told me something that was really traumatic and awful about her past and then assumed I didn't want her anymore because of it. I was in shock and she ran off before I could figure out what to say. Now she won't answer her phone and I can't find her anywhere. I'm worried about her

Henry: Dude that's rough.

Eric: Yeah, man. That sucks. How can we help?

I stopped in the middle of Adventureland where I had unintentionally wandered in my desperate search.

Me: I don't know what I can do. I just ... I can't lose her. I love her. Help. What should I do?

Eric: Where are you? I'm in the parks, I'm coming to you now.

Henry: You have to find her and explain. And soon.

I squeezed my eyes shut, trying not to yell out in frustration. Beside me, an elderly woman was quietly enjoying an asparagus skewer from Bengal Barbecue, as if the whole world wasn't in chaos.

Me: I KNOW. I need to fix this. But I don't know where she lives. I'm in Adventureland right now.

Henry: How do you not know where Leah lives? Haven't you been together for a while now?

Me: It's complicated. She has a past, and she's had to keep things from me for her safety and mine. I get it. But all I know is she lives in an inn nearby with her aunt

Henry: I'm on it. I have some friends in the area who can help. Stand by.

I breathed a sigh of relief. Someone was going to do something. Someone was going to help me find her.

Just then, I noticed Eric striding towards me, concern etched on his face. I stood to greet him, giving him a quick hug that included a bit of a tighter squeeze than normal. It was grounding to have him there, to know I wasn't alone. To know that someone could help me walk through everything that had just happened.

As we sat back down on the painted stone bench, Eric tossed me a sympathetic look. "I'm so sorry, man. I know what Leah means to you."

I swallowed. His condolences sounded too much like what someone said when things were over.

"She's everything to me," I choked out. "I told her how I felt tonight. All of it. And she … she has secrets. Ones I don't fault her for, but it's bad. And she assumed the worst about me, thinking I couldn't love her beyond the bruises she hid under her brave façade."

Unshed tears burned behind my eyes. It stung that she didn't trust me, didn't understand the depth of what I felt for her, or how fully committed I was to *us*.

Eric gazed out into the bustling crowd, lost in thought. I looked up at Penny, the green lucite elephant once meant for Disneyland Paris but now housed above the Jungle Cruise, posing as an import. Leah loved waving hello to Penny every time we walked through

Adventureland. My chest tightened and a full-on, unhinged sob threatened to alert everyone around us that I was falling apart in the happiest place on earth.

Finally, Eric spoke.

"You love her more than Sadie."

It wasn't a question. I leaned forward, resting my elbows on my knees and clasping my nervous hands together before turning to look at Eric. He waited patiently. People often dismissed Eric as some ego-driven, overly self-confident alpha male who didn't understand the nuance of human emotion, but that was just the armor he wore on the outside. Those who got to know him knew better. He had a way of reading people, and he was straightforwardly blunt about what he saw. Not everyone liked hearing what he had to say, but it was usually accurate.

I appreciated the hell out of him, this person who had always seen what was below the surface, just like he was seeing the truth of my allegiance to Leah.

I took a deep breath, admitting what I'd already known since the moment I'd met Leah, since the second she'd unexpectedly stepped into my world and finished my Snow White fountain story.

I couldn't stop the insane smile that tugged at the corners of my mouth when I thought of her.

"I do love her more than Sadie. Leah brings more sunshine than a Dole whip float in the Tiki Room on a hot afternoon. There's something about her, a quiet fierceness. It's like she knows what she wants, but the world has stolen something from her, so she doesn't know how to take it."

I paused and swallowed, remembering all that she had told me this evening.

"And yet she's a fighter, choosing to be brave and love and live brightly even when she's been placed in an impossible situation. I aspire to her level of compassion for her followers, especially how vulnerable she is with them, to the extent that she can do so safely. Leah is the Alice to my Marc Davis, completing me in ways I don't think I will ever fully understand."

"Wow, that's great, man. I don't think I ever heard you talk about Sadie that way, and you guys were together for what felt like an eternity." Eric paused, a thoughtful expression fixed on his face as he observed people pouring out of the exit of the Jungle Cruise. "Imagine that ... a love like Alice and Marc." He turned his focus to me. "We gotta go get your girl back."

Just then, my phone buzzed, and I dug it out of my pocket, hardly able to believe what was on the small screen.

Henry: I have her address. She lives with her aunt Meredith Hart at the Cabana Inn across the street from the parks.

All the air left my lungs at once as Eric, who had leaned over slightly to read the text, slapped me on the back twice and simply declared, "Let's go get your Leah."

As we stepped into the cool air-conditioned lobby of the Cabana Inn, I immediately looked around for signs of Leah. The logical part of my brain told me that of course there wouldn't be signs. Why would she broadcast her presence when she so desperately needed to hide it? But I couldn't help myself.

A woman in her mid-40s with auburn hair and gentle eyes addressed us politely.

"Welcome to the Cabana Inn. May I help you?"

I tried not to look as crazy as I felt, thinking Leah was so near, but not being able to see her. I didn't want to be seen as one more person Leah's family had to hide her from.

I cleared my throat. "Uh, yeah, hi. My name is Lucas, would you happen to know if Meredith Hart is available?"

Her eyebrows shot up, clearly not expecting that question. Her expression quickly fell into one of wariness and suspicion, and I internally cringed.

"Why yes, I'm Meredith. What can I do for you?"

"I'm Lucas. Lucas Barsotti." I lowered my voice, despite the empty lobby, in case anyone was within hearing distance. "Has Leah told you about me?"

Her eyes grew wider than the Pixar Pal-A-Round.

"You're LucaDisNerd."

I smiled at the reference to my online persona, grateful that she'd heard of me at least. Maybe it was a start.

"Yes. I am. Is Leah ..." I paused, fearful of how she might answer. "Is she here?"

Meredith was quiet for a moment, studying me from top to bottom before swinging her eyes over to Eric's imposing 6' 3" frame.

"Who is this?" The suspicion was back in her voice, and I sighed inwardly. I'd known this wouldn't be easy.

"My good friend Eric. Maybe you've heard of him, he's a content creator too like me, EricOnTheHunt?"

I looked at her expectantly, while Eric, the suave gentleman that he was, extended his hand for her to shake. She clasped his hand hesitantly. He smiled in the disarming way that had charmed countless women on social media and made hundreds try to slide into his DMs.

Not that he necessarily sought that, at least not anymore. Eric just had a way about him.

"Nice to meet you, Meredith," he said, his voice warm as a summer day.

She flushed, withdrawing her hand. "Yes. Well. Alright then." She paused for a moment, clearly weighing her options.

Then she sighed.

"Leah's told me about you, Lucas. But you'll forgive me if I don't bestow trust easily." She set her palms on the counter and leaned towards us, her body language communicating her fierce protectiveness.

I instantly respected her more for her obvious concern for my Leah.

"I understand. But ... Leah and I, we ... well, we told each other how we feel tonight. And then Leah shared—"

I broke off and looked at Eric, knowing I couldn't say too much in front of him. Not without Leah's permission.

"She shared what happened," I continued. " Why she's ... here." I looked at Meredith knowingly, hoping she would understand the situation.

Luckily, Meredith was as bright as Leah and picked up the nuance in my words without me having to spell things out.

She nodded carefully.

"I thought she might open up to you. She told me that you were close. I assumed eventually she would need to say something. I'm honestly surprised she hadn't told you before now, but you know Leah. She's"—Meredith's eyes shifted to Eric and back—"careful. You understand."

"I do. But somehow Leah and I got ... disconnected tonight. She was upset. She misunderstood me, and now I just need to talk to her to set things straight. Could you tell her that I'm here, please? Her phone is off and I just need ..."

I looked down, taking a few deep, shaky breaths before I brought my chin back up.

"Please. I just need to talk to Leah."

Meredith's facial features moved from puzzled to horrified. Just like that, I knew what she was going to say. The weight of it hit me in the gut like a cannon from the Jolly Roger, my stomach pitching violently.

"She never turns her phone off, Lucas. Not ever. And she's not here. I thought she was in the parks with you." She began frantically moving around the room, collecting her keys and her phone and calling out to someone in the back to watch the front desk, all while my world collapsed to nothing in an instant.

Meredith stopped in front of me, sliding a cross-body bag over her shoulder. Seeing my shocked, pale face, she locked her eyes with mine and uttered commanding words I wanted to believe.

"Listen to me. We. Won't. Let. Him. Win. Leah is strong. But she's angered Max by hiding for so long. If you love Leah like I think you do, there isn't time for hesitation. She needs us. Now."

I nodded, taking a deep breath. Eric too gave a sharp nod, finally understanding what was at stake. Like the friend I knew him to be, he was all in.

I texted Henry on our way out the door to Meredith's SUV.

We need another favor from those friends of yours. Now.

Chapter 12

Leah

My head was fuzzy as I blinked my eyes open, my eyelids scraping my corneas like sandpaper. Darkness folded in around me, tucking me into an oblivious state that terrified me as I tried to orient myself, lying on my side in utter confusion.

My mind searched for memories. For how I got here, wherever "here" was. Something crawled across my forehead and I brought my arm up to swipe at it, and that's when I realized my arms were tied behind my back. I shook my head violently before shifting awkwardly in an attempt to sit up, each motion of my body amplifying the throbbing in my head and making me groan.

I remembered the submarines.

Yes. Those.

Blue water.

Colorful reefs.

A hand grasping my arm.

I gasped.

Oh no.

No, no, no.

Tears streamed down my face as everything came flooding back to me.

Max gripping my arm tightly, pulling me close until his hot breath hissed in my ear.

"Found you, Leah Bird."

I had started to let out a shriek, but his mouth covered mine to quickly stifle it. He'd pressed into the fake kiss, his anger cutting my lip on my teeth. I could still taste the combination of metallic taste of blood and stale cigarettes, and it made my stomach lurch.

Releasing my mouth, Max wrapped his arms around me tightly in a pretend embrace, whispering words only I could hear. "Don't try to fight me, Leah bird. I know where that *boy* you've been dancing with lives, and if you don't come with me quietly and convincingly, I will end him."

I shook my head, trying to dislodge the memory of him pulling me hurriedly but discreetly through the park and out the front gates. The whole time I had searched around frantically for a friend in security who I could alert to the situation, but none appeared. It was like Max had known exactly how to manipulate the system to get what he needed. Like he always did.

As my eyes adjusted to my dim surroundings, I realized that I was in some sort of closet, surrounded by shoes and hanging clothes. The scent was terrifyingly familiar, earthy with a hint of spice, a unique scent I would know anywhere.

It was Max's closet.

He'd locked me in his closet.

I took a shaky breath and tried moving my hands against the plastic zip-tie restraints at my back. They didn't budge, no matter what I did to try to loosen them.

More memories come screaming back to me. The nonchalant way Max said goodnight to the exit security guards, none of whom I had recognized. The superior smirk on his face as he walked me toward his car parked in a nearby motel lot. The evil words he whispered about what he was going to do to me as he banged my head against the car's trunk before shoving me in it.

That's when the blackness seeped over my world, taking all hope with it.

As I sat in Max's closet surrounded by the horrifying, suffocating scent of his cologne, I wondered how. How had he managed to get into the park when he was banned? He knew right where to find me, and I wasn't even on my live.

I suppose it didn't matter. Having the answers didn't change my situation.

I shifted my body so that I could sit upright and lean against the wall, facing the door. Immediately, a shooting pain radiated from my head throughout my body. I groaned.

I had to find a way out.

There was no way Max was going to let me go this time. After what he whispered in my ear? I knew he was furious about me and Lucas and had every intention of ending us.

Ending me.

Permanently.

I squeezed my eyes shut.

Think, Leah. You've escaped before. You can do it again.

I huffed out a breath and shook my head in disbelief, irritated at my internal optimism. That was what had gotten me into this mess, believing that I could have more than I deserved. And last time I hadn't been tied up and locked in a closet; the only restraint back then had been the chokehold of fear that shadowed my everyday life with Max.

But Lucas ...

Lucas was out there. While he probably didn't want anything to do with me, the reality was that I couldn't help but love him, regardless of how he felt toward me. How was I going to warn him about Max? He needed to lay low. He needed to take precautions. But how was I going to tell him when I was tied up in a closet?

I hated myself for bringing all this into his life. Lucas was my safe harbor, and I'd lured him out into the storm.

I felt the drops of my tears hitting my lap before I'd even noticed I had let them fall. Lucas called me a princess, but I was really more like the secret evil villain that you trusted until they turned on you. I was like an accidental Hans.

The sorrow in my chest grew, engulfing me in a wave that threatened to make me give up. My whole body shook with each silent sob, each desperate wail that I suppressed. I wouldn't let my captor hear what would only bring him pleasure.

I was the worst person for Lucas. He really did deserve so much better than me.

But then in my head, I heard his voice, almost as if he spoke directly to me.

No, Leah. You are more worthy than you'll ever know. You are not a villain. You are the woman that I love, more beautiful than Snow White and more brilliant than Professor Ludwig von Drake on his best day. I am honored to love you. Don't you dare ever insult my favorite Disney historian ever again.

A smile crept its way onto my face despite the darkness of my current situation as the truth washed over me.

I was fully loved, just as I was. Flaws and all.

Lucas loved me, or at least he had loved me. Before all of this.

I mulled over the events on the Motor Boat Cruise pier, picking apart the chaotic events of the evening until I could make sense of what had actually happened instead of the bizarre story I had told myself about who Lucas was and what he wanted.

That was the moment I realized he had never taken back what he said about loving me. He hadn't even tried to end things.

The shock made me sit up straighter. I hadn't allowed him to talk or given him the chance to reject me. I had just run from him out of fear of rejection and of the pain of losing him. Didn't he chase after me as I fled Fantasyland?

I hadn't really given him a chance to respond.

The truth was almost as painful as the injuries Max had inflicted upon my skull.

If I hadn't run—if I had truly *trusted* Lucas with all of my ugly past—then maybe I wouldn't be where I was, caught up again in Max's twisted world. Maybe Lucas could have helped me. How, I don't really know. But he was *Lucas;* he would have found a way.

And loved me through it all.

This I knew to my core: Lucas was not my knight in shining armor, but my partner by my side. He called me princess, but not to condescend or to stereotype me as some helpless female. No, he meant it as my parents had intended when they chose it. Princess Leia, a brave warrior who loved deeply and fiercely, and was not afraid to do what needed to be done.

It was this thought that bolstered my resolve to escape. I was not helpless. I refused to spend the rest of my days as a victim.

I had to get out of this closet.

For Lucas, yes.

But even more, for *Leah*.

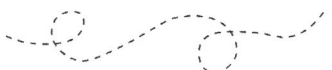

Lucas

42 Walcrest Way. Police are notified and are on their way.

If the situation wasn't so dire, I would have laughed. It was all too close to the address in Sydney that Dory had to remember in Pixar's *Finding Nemo* to find Marlin's missing son. The irony was not lost on me. But as I stared down at the words Henry had texted to me just moments before, humor wasn't my primary emotion.

It was relief.

We had a location, a chance to find my Leah.

"We have an address!" My words came out in a desperate sob, echoing loudly in the worn interior of Meredith's old '93 Jeep Grand Cherokee.

"Whose address?" Eric asked, pulling up his navigation app to punch the address into his phone.

"Henry says it's Max's last known address. Leah might not be there. He might have taken her somewhere else—somewhere less obvious. I don't know. But we have to try."

Meredith was quiet, even as she glanced at the screen Eric had placed in her phone mount to follow the new route. She pursed her lips and shook her head.

"No, he's there. He's too cocky, he probably thinks he's fooling everyone by doing what's most obvious. Max underestimates everyone around him, it's one of his greatest flaws. He believed if he manipulated, diminished, and controlled Leah enough, she would never leave him. But he never saw her inner strength, what her parents could see from the very first moment they looked at her. That's why they named her what they did, not just because they were huge Star Wars nerds. When her dad looked at her, he saw a beautiful fighter who could save the world if she wanted to. I remember him telling me about the day she was born, and how he held her in his arms in the hospital and saw the truth of who she was, and that there was only ever one choice of what to name her."

I took all of this in while staring anxiously out the front window watching the yellow lines slide one by one next to the Jeep's hood. Wringing my hands, I leaned forward, elbows on my knees as if my own forward motion could move us faster toward our goal.

"Princess Leah," I whispered, almost imperceptibly, "we're coming for you. Hang on. Don't stop fighting."

Leah

Wanting to escape and doing so were two very different things. After I had decided to make a way out, the aching blow to my head had other ideas. I drifted in and out of consciousness, unable to make any progress toward escape. Did I have a concussion?

I couldn't seem to fight the sleep that kept pulling me under, into a dream world infiltrated by the demons that plagued me. Startling awake, the remnants of these nightmares crept around the closet like specters of the Shadow Man, plucking at my worst fears and amplifying every horrible memory of my time with Max.

But then there was Lucas, the sweet memory I clung to in my concussion-addled half-aware state in the depths of Max's musty old closet.

Lucas had shown me that none of what Max did was love, that it was only Max's ego parading around as affection, pretending as much as Ursula did when she used Ariel's voice to become Vanessa and trap Prince Eric in *The Little Mermaid*. She had all the right words, said all the right things the right way, and he was completely and utterly fooled, captivated by her spell until it was almost too late.

I wish I had seen the Vanessa signs earlier. Maybe it wouldn't have made me erect the walls around my heart higher and more formidable than the stronghold that Sleeping Beauty Castle represented.

I sighed, tired of fighting to stay conscious when sleep was so much easier. I let the darkness pull me under again, but this time my dreams were filled with light.

It was Lucas.

The dream Lucas resembled the real-life version because all I could feel were his arms secured around me, embracing me tightly on his lap and whispering something about holding on and fighting and that he was coming for me. His warm hand gently cradled my throbbing head to his chest, and I could hear his heartbeat steadily *thump thump thump*ing in my ear.

He quietly hummed "Stay Awake" like he had done not so long ago as we cocooned together in Fowler's harbor, and I pulled back to find his blue eyes misty and imploring me to stay with him. To stay and not let oblivion take me away from him.

I shivered at the intensity of his gaze, of the love and fear of losing that love warring with one another as he leaned in closer, pausing only when his lips were a hairsbreadth from my own. There he lingered, my dream Lucas, so real I swore I could feel his warmth on my skin, each of us aware of the very real possibility that this might be our last shared breath together.

And then he spoke.

"Leah, *my* Leah. I love you so desperately. There is no great, big, beautiful tomorrow without you. I will find you. I will never stop searching for you."

I could only look on as the last piece of my heart I had been holding onto, that I'd been keeping safe "just in case," slowly transferred from my chest to his. Tears found new paths down my cheeks as every last defense I'd employed to keep Lucas out came crumbling down.

He saw me. Not the me I projected to the world, or the me that was safe for him to see. Lucas saw *me*. Perfectly imperfect, shattered and glued back together, hopelessly broken *me*. And it was *that me* that he loved.

And it was that me who loved *him*, too.

Sobs wracked my chest as I fought to take it all in, curling myself back against his chest, needing to be held by the man who would search for me even if all he had was a glass slipper of hope as to where I may be. He *would* find me. I knew it.

I gathered myself together, taking a deep fortifying breath as I listened again to the comforting *thud thud thud* coming from Lucas's chest.

Except it wasn't coming from his chest.

And it was getting louder.

I woke up, pulling myself up from the dirty floor as I fought to make sense of my tangled thoughts.

They were footsteps, not heartbeats.

A click of a key, a squeak of protesting hinges, and a bright, blinding light suddenly landed me face to face with every nightmare I'd ever had.

Max looked down at me with a sneer.

"Have a nice nap, little bird?"

Chapter 13

Lucas

The darkened windows of the house perched on the side of the cliff overlooking the sea revealed no clue as to what was going on inside its walls.

A seagull swooped by the faded maroon hood of Meredith's Jeep, and the unseen surf crashing below seemed to reiterate the urgency of our situation, as if it didn't already reverberate through every bone in my body.

She was in there. She had to be.

As soon as the tires stopped rolling, I moved to open the Jeep's passenger side door. Eric stopped me, grabbing my arm from his location in the backseat.

"No, Lucas! We need to wait for the police. We don't know what that psycho is doing in there or how he might be armed. We can't just go rushing in there."

"He's right," Meredith chimed in. "We need to wait for help, to have a plan, and think this through."

I leaned back in my seat and ran a frustrated hand through my hair, rumpling it for the thousandth time this hour. Leah was so close, and she needed me, but I knew they were right. This wasn't the time to risk getting hurt or, worse, getting Leah hurt because I acted with my heart instead of my head.

I blew out an impatient breath.

"But why aren't the police here yet? Shouldn't they have beaten us here?" I shot off a text to Henry, asking him the same thing. I watched the three little dots bounce up and down on his screen, indicating that he was typing before his reply came a few moments later.

I read it aloud. "Henry says the police are on their way, dispatched from the station, but there was a massive 20-car pileup on the Five that has gridlocked traffic."

I closed my hands into fists, the waiting ripping me apart like the old foam seat cushions below me. Didn't every second count when it came to getting Leah away from this lunatic?

Meredith had a death grip on the steering wheel, internally mulling over the situation. Eric saw my distress and set a hand on my shoulder to keep me grounded.

"This house isn't exactly in downtown LA, bro. It might take a little time for them to get here."

I stared out the car window at the solemn, unassuming white house with the dark ocean crashing behind it. The scent of the sea swirled around us as a sudden gust of wind rocked the Jeep, making me think of what Leah could be enduring at this very moment at the hands of that madman. The wind whistled around us, begging me to do something. *Anything*.

That thought set me in motion.

"That's not good enough."

I flew out of the car door and dashed toward the eerily hushed house. I could hear Meredith and Eric calling out my name, begging me to come back, that it wasn't safe, but all rational thought had disappeared, replaced with a single phrase: *Find Leah*.

I slowed my pace only when I reached the front door. Rationality reappeared, my mind screaming at me to think this through and be careful—not for my sake but for Leah's. Who knew what that man was doing to her, and if I went flying through the door, how he might hurt her before I could get close enough to stop him.

Breathing heavily, I closed my eyes and forced myself to think. He would be expecting me via the front entryway. Likely even had an alarm system. I needed to find another way in. More importantly, I needed to figure out where he was holding Leah.

Creeping around the side of the house, I peeked into the window and spied what seemed to be a living room. Decked out in black leather furniture and stark white walls, the ironic dichotomy of light versus dark wasn't lost on me. Of course, this bastard would have a pristine home, to keep up appearances. Everything about the place oozed success and order.

No, not order. *Control*.

I scanned the room but saw no evidence of Max or Leah. Ducking under the window frame, I moved as stealthily as possible to the next window, and then the next, my desperation growing with each empty room I passed.

"Leah, where are you?"

The whispered plea poured out of me as the hopelessness of my situation sank into my bones, like the fog that crawled in from the ocean, enveloping me on all sides.

The back patio of the house was tucked underneath a second-floor balcony. Reaching it, I approached a set of French doors from the left side, hoping for just a glimpse of Leah, a tiny bit of pixie dust to aid my flight to the woman I loved. There was a tiny sliver of a view between the frame and a roller shade that had been pulled down for privacy, the necessity of which I didn't want to consider. And there, in that sliver of perspective, sat my Leah.

Tied to a chair. Looking straight at me with panic in her eyes.

My attention was immediately pulled to her pale neck, the one I had kissed so gently under the stars. The one my hand had journeyed up before tangling in her soft, golden hair. The one that held up her astutely brilliant mind that understood Disney history—understood me—better than anyone I'd ever known.

Because there, held to that length of skin I loved so well, was a shining blade.

Max had seen me.

And his dark eyes told me I would never hold Leah again.

Leah

I vaguely remembered Max dragging me out of the closet and down the hallway. Somewhere along the way, I had succumbed to the darkness again, because when I woke up, I was in a hard wooden armchair facing Max who was perched in his own vintage chair, sipping what could only be a Scotch Mist.

He did it to mock me, poking fun at what he called my "delusional love of Walt Disney," just like he had when we'd been together. Walt's preferred drink of choice was Black and White Scotch whisky with lemon peel over ice, and even though Max hated Scotch, he had always kept it on hand to drink when he was angry with me.

I watched as his Adam's apple bobbed with each swallow. His eyes never left mine as he drank deeply of the strong spirits, observing my reaction, knowing that I knew what it all meant.

Max believed he owned me. To him, I was a trophy as much as any of the dusty paintings lining the hallways of his pompously overdone home.

I had been so impressed by his lifestyle when I first met him. He seemed to have so much that I had only dreamed of, and he had wanted to share it all with me. He bought me expensive gifts, flew me to exotic destinations for vacation, and flaunted his success at every opportunity. I was starstruck by his charisma, clinging to his approval like the lost safari held to the tree while fleeing the charging rhino on the Jungle Cruise.

That Max and the one before me were one and the same; he just hid his dark side well. No one would suspect it of him, the way he enjoyed tearing me down piece by piece, the secrets he held close. How dangerous he truly was.

"You can't look away from me, can you, little bird?" Max smirked, taking another swig from the glass in his hand. "I know you missed me. I can tell by the way you're trembling."

Shock at his absurd assessment raced through me before shifting into stark realization. This was a game to him. A sick, sad game that I was destined to lose, but a game all the same. Disgust left me speechless.

"Cat got your tongue, little bird?" Max set his glass down with a soft clink on the glass side table before leisurely standing up and sauntering towards me. "Perhaps I should loosen it up for you." He moved behind me, running his once-tempting hands over my shoulders as he passed, reminiscent of the first time we met. A very different kind of shiver ran down my spine than it had that day back in the cafe.

Max set his palms heavily on my shoulders before leaning down close to my ear and lingering for a moment, his heated breath causing my body to shake even more violently as all the memories of my old life came crashing down around me.

Max chuckled as he felt each tremor, absorbing them as if they fueled his cruelty.

"Oh, are you scared, little bird? You should be. I saw you with him. And he had the audacity to touch what is *mine*."

With those words, his hands slipped around my neck, finding their way to the top button of my vintage dress, slipping each one out of its secure fastening, slowly exposing the pale skin of my throat to his fingertips. He ran his consummately tidy fingers over the newly bared skin, and I let out an involuntary whimper.

I squeezed my eyes tight as he unbuttoned another button, and then another, trying to escape at least mentally if I could not physically.

"UNAUTHORIZED ENTRY. SOUTH PERIMETER."

I gasped as Max pulled his hands away, reaching for his phone.

My heart galloped in my chest as hope entered the room.

The security alarm.

Someone was here.

Someone would stop him.

Relief flooded my system, causing the tears I'd been holding back for so long to race rapidly down my face toward the floor.

Sickeningly, Max didn't look angry or upset that his game was interrupted. Instead, a sudden glee altered his visage while he peered at the security camera's live feed on his phone.

"Looks like your boyfriend has come to play. Let's give him a show, little bird."

All thoughts of escape fled in that millisecond.

No. Not Lucas.

All of the time I tried to keep him safe, and it all led to this: to me leading him directly into Max's darkness. All because I selfishly wanted Lucas's light.

I put my unaffected mask back in place, trying to pretend as if none of it mattered. If I could go to that place in my mind, maybe I could convince Max that Lucas didn't mean anything to me. It was the only possible way to keep him safe.

As Max slid back across the room to me, I threw out what I hoped was a casual statement.

"Oh that guy? Yeah, we broke up. A while ago, actually. He's kind of obsessed with me, but trust me, it's not going to happen." I swallowed hard, choking out the next part. "I could never really get over you, anyway."

I felt bile rising in my throat with each false word, but then I thought about Lucas. This was all for Lucas. So I ended my performance with what I knew he wanted to hear.

"How could I want to be with anyone else?"

Max burst out laughing and then started to applaud slowly, a sinister grin creeping over his face.

"Well done, little bird. Of all the lies you've told to elude me, I'm pretty impressed by that one. Because it's what you *should* be saying, maybe with an apology for ever having been with anyone else. But the evidence doesn't lie." He shoved his phone in my face, the video feed showing Lucas coming around the side of the house and peeking in each window. "You can't convince me that this guy doesn't think he still has a claim on you. We're going to have to do something about that."

Max walked calmly to a wooden case sitting on top of the ostentatious fireplace mantle. Winds from an incoming storm were whipping down the flue, replacing the silence with a soft whistling that echoed throughout the room.

He opened the lid of the case and pulled out what could only be some kind of hunting or fishing knife, its blade catching the light as he angled it toward me.

"Shall we play with your 'ex' boyfriend, Leah? He looks like someone who likes to have some fun." Max sneered, walking first to the French doors directly in front of me and throwing the lock open before sauntering back behind me, knife in hand. I felt its cool steel kiss the soft skin under my chin, and I slid my eyelids closed, wanting to picture Lucas in my mind, if this was all that was left of my time on Earth. Wanting to envision him somewhere safe, far from here and the mess I'd made of both our lives.

"UNAUTHORIZED ENTRY. LOWER WEST PATIO."

My eyes flew open, realizing that was the very door Max had just unlocked. And sure enough, there in the gap between the door and the shade were the blue eyes that had saved me in more ways than I could possibly recount.

My Lucas.

He was *here*.

He hadn't given up on me. I hadn't scared him off.

He'd found me. Even when I believed I wasn't worthy of being found.

I watched with desperation as Lucas took in the situation: Max, with his hand around my throat and a knife pressed against my skin. The buttons on my dress helplessly hung open, telling a story I fiercely wanted to erase from my memory and his, forever. My hands zip-tied behind me, and my legs similarly attached to the legs of my chair.

Even through the barrier of glass, I could hear Lucas growl as he threw open the door and sprinted into the room.

But Max wasn't about to give up control that easily.

"I'd stop right there if you don't want to stain this flawless vintage Vogue dress. Or it's model."

Lucas

I froze in place, the words Max flung my way finding purchase where my heart connected with my head. But while he had my ears, my eyes belonged only to Leah, asking her a silent, imploring question.

She knew what I was asking, and her mouth almost imperceptibly formed the words "I'm okay."

Relief flooded my system, joining the adrenaline that had not loosened its grip on me since Leah had left the safety of my arms hours before.

That monster had not stolen more from her than he'd previously taken. I had not failed Leah.

At least, not yet.

Max was growing impatient, watching our exchange with irritation.

"Well, isn't this a touching reunion? A bit more tragedy than comedy, though, considering there is only one way this will end. If Leah won't be with me, she won't be with anyone, I'm afraid." Shifting his body closer to Leah and leaning in close, I heard Max faintly whisper in her ear, "And you know too much."

My blood boiled. His words had held Leah captive for far too long. She deserved exquisite castle sunrises and a million fireworks dessert parties surrounded by those who loved her. Not this. Never this.

My heart shattered at the idea that Leah would never get to share the full extent of her brilliance with the world, all because this sociopath convinced her she was less than who she was—that she was not, and never would be, good enough.

And that's when something inside me snapped.

I rushed toward Max, my gaze focused on the critical spot where the razor-sharp blade held the fate of Leah's life. He startled, cutting her throat. A line of red appeared, trickling down her skin, staining her future. Her eyes faded. Her eyelids shuttered. And I looked on helplessly as her body slumped to the side.

"Leah! No!!" I lunged for Max, intent on pushing him away.

Away from my strong princess.

Away from my found treasure.

Away from my perfectly imperfect love.

Just as my hand gripped Max's arm to pull him away from Leah, the glass behind me inexplicably shattered. Max suddenly fell to the floor, pulling me with him, until we landed side by side. It was then I saw the bloom of red spreading across his chest, and heard the rasping of his breath as his cold, dark eyes met my own.

Wrenching away from his grasp, I sobbed out Leah's name, arching my body up to try to see her better, begging her to respond. How had this happened? She couldn't possibly be gone! I called her name again and again, but she didn't move.

It felt like swimming underwater, this surreal moment where I was watching every dream I'd held fade away like the ending of a film. My world had forever gone dark the moment Leah fell to the side.

I laid back down, defeated.

She was gone.

I could hear others shouting, but I shoved the sounds away. Their words didn't matter.

Nothing mattered now. Not really. Not without *her*.

My Leah.

Her name pressed into my shattered heart, a piercing pain radiating out of my chest into my paralyzed body. The coldness of the blade that had taken Leah from me seemed to pervade my skin, chilling me to the bone.

I was lost. Gone. Finished.

The voices in the room suddenly amplified in volume. Someone was screaming at me.

"Lucas! LUCAS! Are you okay? Lucas!!"

I saw Eric and Meredith move in behind SWAT team members, anxiously racing toward me and Leah, respectively. My gaze drifted again to what was left of Leah, but I couldn't see her well from where I had fallen behind her chair.

The knot in my chest twisted tighter, knowing I had failed her. That I'd been too late.

Max had gotten what he wanted.

But no, he hadn't. Not really. Because as the fog lifted from my mind, I found him lying on the floor next to me, his life draining away with every moment that passed.

I studied Max with a numb lack of compassion. His eyes had gone glassy with the blood loss. His mouth opened and closed frantically, trying to speak, but I couldn't quite make it out. I leaned in closer, trying to decipher what would undoubtedly be his last words, judging by the bullet in his chest.

But when I got close, Max's countenance changed, transforming from agony to disturbing delight.

As he slipped the knife into my stomach, I finally understood what he was trying to say.

"If I can't have her, neither can you."

Chapter 14

Lucas

"... and to our right are the windows for Marc and Alice Davis."

A sweet voice I knew I'd never hear again wound its way around me as I swam in the darkness.

Where was I? Was I laying down on Main Street?

No, that didn't make sense...

"Remember how we told everyone about their 44-year love story, having fallen in love while working on Sleeping Beauty? We argued about who was the better animator, and I pointed out that it was not Alice's fault she wasn't allowed to become one because women's options were so limited back then. And you said if it had been me I would have found a way to be one anyway."

Tinkling laughter followed.

Leah.

How I ached for her voice to be real and not just in my imagination.

Maybe heaven was just being on Main Street with my true love by my side. If so, sign me up.

"And now we come to the most harrowing part of our journey, our trek across the trolley tracks into the Penny arcade so we can listen to the Welte Orchestrion, cranking out quality tunes since 1907. I remember how you said you could easily play all those at once, and I called you Bert for the rest of the day."

Leah's voice cracked at the end of her sentence like she was holding back tears. Why would she be crying?

"And now we see it, Walt's storybook castle, later called Sleeping Beauty Castle. One that would have been red and black, if Eyvind Earle's sketches had won out when color palettes were proposed. You said you'd love a change to the castle colors, and I argued that the traditional ones were best, and then ..."

I heard Leah swallow a sob.

"... and then you said you would kiss me until I agreed with you."

She exhaled, her breath catching. I wondered what had made her so very sad, especially while recalling such a wonderful memory of us together, being our ridiculous selves next to the castle moat.

"I would now. I would agree with you," Leah murmured, "if you could only hear me say the words."

More sobs. It broke my heart, hearing my Leah so sorrowful.

So I pulled back from the black, gathering all my energy together, and focused on forming the words I knew I needed to say.

My lips were dry. My throat felt like it was on fire. This lighter place was agonizing. But I needed Leah to know I was there, that she wasn't alone in her sadness.

I blinked my heavy eyelids open, not fully seeing anything but Leah, sitting next to me and clinging to my hand.

So I said two words I knew would make her downturned mouth tip up, just trying to stem the flow of tears down her beautiful, beautiful cheeks.

Scraping all my energy reserves, I simply whispered, "I'm listening."

Her head popped up, shock evident in her expression.

"Lucas? Lucas, oh my gosh, *LUCAS!*" Her arms flew around me, and I grunted at the impact of her embrace, suddenly more aware of the extreme pain radiating out below my ribs. But I didn't care. Leah was here.

Leah, who I thought I had failed.

Princess Leah. My Leah.

It was all a blur after that. Leah called in the nurse. A few doctors filtered in and out, checking this and that, asking me questions, shining bright lights in my eyes, and asking me the same questions again and again. When they were done, I had heard enough about my lacerated intestine to last me a lifetime, but I asked Leah to tell me what happened, since everything after Max had stabbed me was fuzzy and unclear.

"Well, according to Eric and Aunt Meredith, the SWAT team sniper took out Max when they saw him cut me with the knife, but I don't remember it because I had passed out at that point from my concussion. The knife did nick me, but it was superficial and didn't even require stitches, thank goodness. You fell behind me with Max when you grabbed him to pull him away from me, and when you both went down, he still had the knife in his hand, and he stabbed you…

"In the intestine, yes, I've heard all about it," I added sardonically.

Leah smiled at my sad attempt at wit, the joy radiating from her warming me from the inside out.

"Yes, he stabbed you while he was still conscious enough to do so, before anyone realized he still had the knife."

"So you are ok? Really? How bad is your concussion?"

"Well, I won't be going on the Incredicoaster anytime soon, but I'm approved for all dark rides. But I am not setting foot in the parks without you, Lucas."

Leah blushed and looked down at our joined hands. "While I've been waiting for you to wake back up, I've been taking you on virtual Disney history tours of the parks, hoping you could hear me, and it would bring you back to me."

"Well, I'd say it was effective. I'm still listening, by the way." I raised my eyebrow at her, our usual exchange for when she's trying to get away with something.

"Huh? For what?" Leah smiled coyly, evading what she knew I wanted from her.

"You know, Leah. Let's hear it. You brought me back from who-knows-where just so I could hear you admit it, so, let's go. Chop chop, little onion."

Leah huffed an irritated sigh before mumbling under her breath, "I guess red and black wouldn't look too awful on the castle."

I smiled at her clever attempt to thwart my request.

"What was that? I couldn't hear you, Princess Leah. Could you speak up? I'm wrapped up in a hospital gown. It's pretty much like being the mummy in the Haunted Mansion, you know, all bundled up. It affects my hearing. Or whatever."

"It's the old man who can't hear and the mummy who can't speak, and you know it, Mr. obsessed-with-Marc-Davis-gags." Leah laughed, and the sound was better than any park soundtrack I'd ever heard.

"Oh, well, in that case, I'm the old man, and you're the mummy." I alter my voice to sound toothless and haggard. "*Shpeak* up, dearie. I can't hear you *shay* how I'm right."

Leah stood up and cleared her throat, preparing for her oration. I grinned at her antics, falling in love with her all over again with each straightening of her clothes and tuck of her hair.

Speaking loudly and clearly, she used Walt-like storytelling gestures as she proclaimed, "I, LeahMetotheMagic, do so solemnly swear that Disneyland's castle..."

She paused, then surprised me by leaning over the bed, gently running a hand up my chest before cupping my jaw and bringing her lips close to my own. I held my breath, waiting for her next move, before she finally whispered, "... is where I want to be with you, LucaDisNerd, forever."

I instantly forgave her for reneging on our deal. She sealed her sworn oath with a kiss that was sweeter than a Mickey bar topped with a churro, and wrapped in the promise of every great, big beautiful tomorrow we would make together.

Chapter 15

Lucas

Four months later

I balanced my phone in one hand as I held on tightly to Leah with my other, smiling to myself at how her hand always found mine, even while we both focused on our work of live streaming. She was never obligated to hold my hand, but she often chose to, not afraid to show the world that we were together.

I think it gave her a sense of power, of finally getting to make her own choices and to be open about who she was and what she wanted.

And hey, if she wanted to use me for that, who was I to say no? At that thought, my grin grew larger, a fact that didn't escape Leah.

"I don't know what is so funny about C.V. Wood shaking down Main Street renters for more money after they moved in via his associate Bob Burns. Heck, even Bob Gurr called him a con man. Wood was not a good guy." She cocked her head at me, The hint of a smile on her lips. "Why are you grinning at me like the Cheshire Cat, Lucas?"

I tried to reel in my delight, afraid she would get suspicious. Panicking that I would give everything away, I turned to address my online friends instead of my love at my side. This earned me an irritated huff from Leah.

"What do you think, everyone? Should a man who is in the Happiest Place on Earth with the woman he loves be free to smile without being accused of mental instability?"

HenryAroundtheWorld: Absolutely, mate. Especially when she's as beautiful as Leah

I bristled, even though I knew Henry didn't mean anything by it. He was a notorious flirt. His charming English accent usually didn't hurt his cause in that arena, either.

Leah was peeking at my chat over my shoulder, and, wanting to rile me, chose to flirt right back.

"Why thank you, Henry. That's so sweet of you to say."

My head swiveled, and I found her grinning at me and tossing a wink in my direction. I leaned in close and whispered in her ear, "Flip your camera around so they can't see."

Her eyes twinkled as she exclaimed effusively to her chat, "Hey, look at how beautiful the Rivers of America are this time of day! Let's just take in the magic for a moment."

As soon as both of our cameras were flipped to a forward-facing view, I grabbed Leah and pulled her in close, my mouth descending on hers even as we both tried to hold our phones steady side-by-side, focused on a view of the sparkling water and the *Mark Twain* floating by. We lost ourselves in the moment, finding each other again and again, in this place where we'd had our first dance together, once upon a time.

I slowly pulled back before dropping gentle kisses up the line of her jaw, working my way up to nuzzle in her hair. I spoke soft and low, rumbling words meant for her ears alone and not the thousands of people listening in on our day.

"You are more beautiful than every golden reflection on the water, Leah. And every word that falls from your lips is driving me *crazy* today." I gave her earlobe a playful nip before pulling back. Gently, I turned her around toward the Rivers of America, maneuvering her to stand in front of me as we took in the beautiful view together. Careful to keep my phone steady for my audience, I glided my free hand around her waist to rest on her stomach, tugging her back against me. I felt her body relax into my own, and we melted into the moment, at peace together in our happy place.

I took a peek back at my chat, and grimaced slightly.

Ms. Pixiedst: *well, we all know what THAT was about, don't we?*

Resortabelle: *oh absolutely & I'm here for it. They deserve all the happiness*

DressingDapperly: *Life goals: Find a girl like Leah to "look at the river" with*

Ohana626: **sigh* I love their love story*

Leah nestled back against me and sighed. "I love it too. Thanks, Ohana."

Having Leah so close was messing with my judgment. But today, I didn't care who saw, or who judged us. We'd come so far from Leah running away from me in fear, and hiding who she really was. I ducked my head down to murmur a question in her ear, one I'd wanted to ask her for so long but was irrationally scared to pose.

Shaking the demons of my past off my shoulders, I took a risk, and asked, "Leah, what do you see?"

She paused for a moment, and my brain started to go in every direction at once. I knew that I shouldn't be afraid to ask Leah what I'd asked Sadie so long ago, but the past sometimes hangs around us like a grim grinning ghost. And the longer she hesitated, the more my fears rose.

But then, everything changed.

"I love that question, Lucas. It really is complex, isn't it? Because on the surface, I see a sunset sparkling on the water, and the *Mark Twain* making slow ripples in its wake. I see tired people across the way, queuing up for the Haunted Mansion. I see ducks trying to find their next meal, and Tom Sawyer's island turning brilliantly gold before our eyes in the waning sun."

I held my breath, waiting for more. Knowing she had more. And my heart soared knowing it was so.

"But it's deeper than that. I see Walt Disney on his 30th wedding anniversary drinking Mint Juleps and slow dancing with Lillian on the decks of the *Mark Twain* to some easy Dixieland jazz. I see him feeling the joy and relief that they'd built Disneyland in a year, alongside celebrating the love he'd built for years with his dear wife. I see the island that he sketched by hand, and the cast of characters in his life who helped bring his dream to life. I see, right here, the culmination of a lifetime of hopes and dreams, all summed up by a simple pristine reproduction sternwheeler gliding through the water."

Tears pricked my eyes. Leah got it. She understood what this place meant, what it represented.

Her chat flew, and I snuggled her closer to me as I read their comments, unable to speak quite yet.

ElsieSnow: *wow, that's beautiful*

MinnieMags: *I'm not crying, you're crying*

BeM1neGaston: *I love the way she sees Disney*

WaltinTime: *And that's why we love you, Leah. You see so much more because you see the history behind it*

Leah gave a nervous chuckle. She didn't know what to do with so much praise, but, with time, she was getting better at believing she was worthy of it.

"Thanks, Pixiecrew! But enough about me. What do you see, Lucas?"

I grinned, gently swaying us back and forth, ambivalent that the motion could be detected in both of our online streams. My whole being wanted to dance with my Princess, the world be damned.

"I see the same, Princess Leah. I see the love Walt had, not only for this park, but for his wife, who was his match in so many ways. She believed in him, even when his ideas seemed impossible and money was scarce. She challenged him, convincing him that Mickey was a much better choice than Mortimer Mouse. And she loved him, so much so that she allowed their backyard to become a railroad because it was what he loved."

"Though she did insist on seeing her garden from her window, hence the tunnel that Walt had to build for the Carolwood Pacific," Leah added with a cheeky grin.

I laughed. "Yes, yes she did. She wasn't afraid to tell him like it was. Like you do for me, and I love it. I love that you feel the freedom of knowing you can own your thoughts and opinions, that you are not afraid to put me in my place. Except, of course, when you're absolutely wrong. Like you are more often than you want to admit."

I added the last with a teasing tone, knowing Leah wouldn't be able to resist responding. My heart rate kicked up in anticipation as she spun around, eyes flashing and indignant, ready to defend herself.

"Listen here, LucaDisNerd, you *know* that I do my research, and it's YOU who too often—"

Her indignant tirade was arrested as I took advantage of our proximity and captured her lips in a gentle, sweet, lingering kiss. She slowly melted in my arms ... or arm, rather, since one of them was still holding a phone focused on the river.

But Leah's phone swung wildly as I kissed the woman who was my match as much as Lillian had been for Walt.

TikiRoomVibes: *whoa, I'm gonna be sick*

KyloFanGirl100: *We interrupt this stream to bring you some random crowd footage as Leah and Lucas share a moment*

DisneeLuv23: *Patience, please Pixiecrew. Leah will be right back!*

RopeDropper93: *Are we going on a ride?*

MinnieMags: *I think we just went on one lol*

I lingered for just a moment more, tasting Leah's mouth one last time before coming back to reality and stepping back, trying to get my racing heart and breathing under control.

Leah leisurely blinked her eyes open, clearly lost in the magic of our connection. As she came back to her surroundings, she let out a small, "Oh!" realizing she was still live streaming and her Pixiecrew has been left in the lurch. Holding the camera up to the entrance of Pirates of the Caribbean, she made her apologies to her online friends.

"So sorry about that, crew. You can blame Lucas. I always do." She gave me a pointed look, and I laughed out loud.

I leaned close to her and rumbled in her ear, "I take full and complete responsibility for that flush in your cheeks, Princess."

This only made Leah blush harder, and I grinned, loving every adorable part of her.

I especially loved that she had no idea what was coming.

I cleared my throat.

"So, LeahMetotheMagic, I know today was your day to pick our activities, but I wonder if you would humor me in indulging in an attraction that we both love, one that has, say, identical chickens and a scandalous past?"

Leah's eyes lit up, and I knew at that moment I had her. She could never resist Pirates.

"That depends," she responded, a coy playfulness lacing her tone. "Do you mean the scandal of how the sculptors didn't listen to Alice Davis and originally made the characters completely anatomically correct, so much so that they had to *saw off* valuable parts of the male characters so that said parts wouldn't be visible under their clothes?"

I laughed out loud. My chat went flying.

Ms. PixieDst: *What? That's hilarious!!*

EricOnTheHunt: *Dude, no. Just... no.*

DisHistorIan: *Yeah, Alice tried to warn them, they didn't listen*

User9798236327846: *I'm dying. I'm dead. No way that actually happened. Omg*

"Well, that was not exactly the scandal I was talking about, but sure. For argument's sake, we'll make it that one. The wait is only 15 min, shall we?"

"Let's do it."

I followed Leah under the Pirates of the Caribbean marquee and into the queue, and that's when the panic started to set in. I grew quiet, only half listening to Leah tell stories about opening day and how they used a battering ram to open the front door during the ceremony. Meanwhile, I was internally going over every detail of my plan.

It was clear Leah had absolutely no idea what was about to happen. But some of my friends in the chat did, and they spoke to me in a sort of code we'd worked out in advance so that no one would suspect.

EricOnTheHunt: *the pirates are placed perfectly*

HenryAroundtheWorld: *Shiver me timbers, Lucas*

I took a deep, steadying breath, inhaling the scent of bromine and nostalgia. With my gaze lingering on the love of my life, I gave them the answer they were waiting for, never more sure of any words I'd ever uttered.

"Bring me that horizon."

Chapter 16

Leah

"This scene here at the beginning," I said, "actually draws from the earlier Rogues Gallery walk-through wax museum concept for Pirates. At one point in the storytelling, you would have come upon pirates burying their loot. You then would have quietly slipped away without being seen into a cypress swamp in the bayou before accidentally stumbling into the Battle for the Defense of New Orleans.

"This is partially why we have the Blue Bayou, though, to be honest, the idea of a boat ride through the bayou started with the Haunted Mansion, with the concept of the house sinking into a swamp. Walt Disney thought they had too many boat rides at the time however, and the house went from moldy and decrepit to pristine on the outside, so the Haunted Mansion boat idea was scrapped, only to be partially revived later for Pirates. I've always thought it somewhat ironic that Walt thought they had too many boat rides *before* Small World and the 1964 New York World's Fair."

I paused, reaching for a sip of my water as the noisy load area buzzed around us. I couldn't put my finger on it, but something just felt *off*. Lucas had gone uncharacteristically quiet during that whole story, when he usually tended to jump in and talk about how the parrot was a nod to the one that was planned for the Captain's Quarters.

My concern kicked in. Maybe I was stepping on his toes, maybe he had wanted to tell the whole story. My old insecurities were back, and I silently chastised myself for not thinking to ask, even though he was always so enthusiastic about me sharing any and all stories when we live streamed together.

Colette thought he just liked to listen to me talk. I told her he was just being a gentleman. Maybe he was doing that now?

There was only one way to find out.

"Lucas, are you okay?"

Lucas startled, throwing a wild expression my way before quickly tucking it away and dropping a calm façade in its place.

My anxiety kicked up a notch. Something was definitely wrong.

"Of course. Who wouldn't be, hearing about pirates and syphilis?" He nervously chuckled, giving me a goofy grin, and I gave him an odd look.

"What are you talking about? That wasn't the story I was telling. Were you not listening? Why are you being weird?"

"You're just now figuring out that I'm weird? Wow, maybe you're not as perceptive as I thought," teased Lucas.

I rolled my eyes.

"Whatever. I see details you miss ALL the time." I gave him a poke with a finger to his chest for good measure, and he took the opportunity to capture my hand and gallantly bring my fingers up to his mouth for a gentle kiss.

My heart fluttered in my chest. Those bread-and-butterflies got me every time.

Wearing a cocky grin, he simply offered up, "We'll see, Leah. We'll see."

I tugged my hand out of his, irritated by his attempt to distract me. "What is that supposed to mean?"

"Line is moving, Princess. Better keep up."

I gave my eyes another roll for good measure, wondering what was up with Lucas. But then the Lafitte's Landing sign caught my eye, and I launched into the story of how it had inspired Eddie Sotto with an entire legend about Jean Lafitte that would have created a tunnel under the Rivers of America before exiting into a hold of a ship on the other side, and how sad it was that we only got bits and pieces of his concept with Pirate's Lair on Tom Sawyer Island, because the president of Disney theme parks at the time, Paul Pressler, had nixed the whole idea.

I was still a little bitter about that, to be honest.

CreativelyColette: *There's also that Jean Lafitte anchor near the river that's been there pretty much since DL opened*

MinnieMags: *And the silversmith shop!*

ElsieSnow: *Is that why there is a ship on the weather vane on the Haunted Mansion?*

"No Elsie, though that's a good guess. The ship is there as an homage to the lost Captain Gore storyline of the early Haunted Mansion scripts. He was a ruthless pirate captain who murdered his wife Priscilla when she found out about his true identity. Then she came back to haunt him, eventually driving him mad. That's why there is a hanging man in the stretching room, it came from that original storyline. But there are many ties to the Haunted Mansion and Pirates since they were developed at the same time, like the bayou boat story I told earlier. And there still are some more recent connections today, like the chairs from Gracey Manor that are from the 2003 movie *The Haunted Mansion*. One is in the attic of the Haunted Mansion, and another has Captain Jack Sparrow sitting on it in the treasure room at the end of this ride."

So caught up in my storytelling, I didn't even realize that we'd reached the front of the line and Lucas had already talked to the Cast Member about sitting in the back row as we usually did. I shuffled to the gate, continuing my stories about the original pastel boats the ride used to have in 1967 because that was all the manufacturer had available at the time, and how they all had names of famous women pirates or at least women's names in French and Spanish, like "Camille."

The gates opened to load, and I stepped carefully into our bateau, sliding over on the tan, water-speckled seat to make room for Lucas.

It was then I noticed he'd ended his live stream and put his phone away, and my concern hit a new peak.

"Hey, why aren't you live?"

He shrugged. "Oh, I sent them all to your chat. I just want to enjoy the ride this time, is all."

I looked at my screen and realized that there was, in fact, double my usual view count. It was well over 3,000 people and growing.

Something wasn't adding up. Maybe he was tired of us being live in the parks together so much.

"Okaaaaay…. Do you want me to end my live too, so we can both just enjoy it, together?"

Lucas suddenly sat up ramrod straight and blurted out an echoing "No!" Some exiting guests turned in our direction, startled at the loud exclamation, assessing the situation and resuming their journey out of the attraction. I looked at Lucas aghast, unnerved by his reaction, and he looked back at me for half a beat before relaxing back into his chill attitude.

"I mean, no, it's totally fine. I love listening to you tell all the history."

He offered me a lopsided, quirky smile. I was not convinced. But as our bateau slipped into the dark water and gently floated past the Yale Gracey fireflies, I relaxed into my storytelling, quietly of course, with my phone tucked in close to keep from irritating the other guests in our boat.

I was just telling everyone about how the Blue Bayou restaurant was modeled after the long-gone Chicken Plantation restaurant when Lucas leaned in close to me, softly tucking my hair behind my ear before wrapping his arm around my shoulder. His lips brushed my earlobe as he whispered hushed words wrapped in his familiar bass timbre. My heart danced like the fireflies that surrounded us. I shivered in anticipation of his next move.

"Leah, do you remember that this was the first ride we ever went on together? You were so distraught that day, and I couldn't make sense of it. There you were, this stunning, confident, and fiercely independent creature who spoke about Disney history like it was the air you breathed, and yet you let me see *you* that day. The real you."

I ducked my head down, embarrassed all over again for how I'd reacted, for how much I'd let my fear rule me and my anxiety take over in front of a complete stranger. Ahead, Beacon Joe plucked out a tune on his banjo, rocking lazily back and forth on his porch in the dim twilight, and we placidly floated forth into the darkness, drifting towards the Jolly Roger skull and crossbones that would warn us about dead men telling no tales.

The darkness was triggering, memories of dark trunks and closets creeping into my thoughts. Those pieces of my former life still haunted me, even though I was safe now, with Lucas. I hunched over and curled into myself as if it could somehow protect me from the past.

But Lucas refused to let me go there. He cupped his palm below my chin and brought my head up and around to meet his eyes, before dropping his hand to clasp my free one, weaving his fingers through mine.

"No, Leah. When we met was not a shameful time. Not at all. That day was when I fell in love with you. I fell hard for your perfectly imperfect self, all wrapped up in a ball of Disney history and a passion for making life more magical for others. Probably because your life was less than magical, though I had no idea to what extent back then."

"Lucas, I—"

"Hold that thought, Princess."

As we slid down the two drops into the ghostly grotto, I thought about how Walt Disney himself insisted on splitting the long down ramp into two separate drops, simply because people wouldn't be expecting the second one, and the surprise would be a grand adventure.

Kind of like Lucas. Bright blue-and-green-lit waterfalls poured down around us as I leaned in close to him this time, needing him to hear me over the persistent sound of splashing water.

"Lucas, I fell in love with you too that day, but I was terrified of it. Terrified of you. I mean, I wasn't terrified of *you*, per se, but rather the idea of you. You were perfect. Handsome. Compassionate. You made me laugh when there wasn't much to laugh about in my life. And you saw me, the real me that I didn't let anyone else see. Because, somehow, I knew you were safe even when I wasn't familiar with that concept anymore."

I paused, remembering I was still holding my phone. I aimed it in the direction of the pirate crew members locked in an eternal battle of chess before swinging it to the other side to capture the captain in his bed studying a map. But as the chat was debating whether or not it was a real human skull above him on the headboard, I squeezed Lucas's hand tighter and whispered, "Honestly, I could never forget our first ride together. It was like I had found a missing piece of myself."

Lucas turned his head and captured my mouth in a quick kiss, reciprocating the sentiment without saying a word. The walls slowly closed in on us as we went through the transition tunnel under the railroad tracks that led into the exterior show building.

Light refracted on the rocks around our bateau, as a pirate with his treasure faced consequences for his greed, but I only had eyes for Lucas. Something about this ride was special; I could feel it.

Lucas's eyes sparkled more than the inky water lapping at our bateau. I cocked my head, wondering why there was a slight glistening there, and feeling my eyes respond in kind.

So this was love.

I knew I loved Lucas, but never had I fully dove into the depth of what it meant until that moment. Knowing how he'd always accepted me. Watched out for me. Rescued me. Cherished me. I couldn't fathom being without him.

"Leah, look. This is my favorite part of this ride. Where the scene moves from a limited view, closed in and predictable, to this wide-open, wild adventure where you're thrown into the action of the Wicked Wench, tossed head-first into the chaos. But we love it because it makes us feel alive."

Suddenly our boat halted its forward motion, with a Cast Member announcing, "Your attention please, for technical reasons our adventure has been temporarily interrupted."

My chat started flying with everyone screaming "Possible Evac!" because they knew getting evacuated from this part of the ride would be an amazing experience.

But then I heard something bizarre. Everyone in the boat in front of us and the boat behind us suddenly started singing the ride's theme song, some even harmonizing in a haunting melody that drifted around me and Lucas like an eerie refrain. I turned and looked over my shoulder at the boat behind us, wondering why everyone was suddenly singing.

And then the lights turned on.

No, not the attraction's work lights. The lights from each and every person's cell phone in both boats, plus the one we were currently floating in. And as their faces were illuminated, I could not believe what I was seeing.

They were all faces that I recognized.

My eyes bounced from face to face, seeing all of our friends and even my Aunt Meredith holding up their cell phone flashlights and singing softly. Colette gave me a little wave, wearing a huge grin from the front seat of the boat behind us, holding her camera instead of a cell phone. She gave a two-fingered Disney point in Lucas's direction, and that's when I saw it.

Lucas, down on one knee inside our tiny seating area, offering me a small black box.

I gasped.

No.

And then I laughed.

Of course. Of course, this is how he would propose. I should have known. I grinned at Lucas, and he returned an even brighter smile of his own.

A few people started whistling and cheering when they saw me finally noticing Lucas. Then they resumed their haunting tune, quieter this time at a low hum so that they could listen. Eric, who had been secretly seated in front of us the whole time, gently loosened the phone from my hand and took over my live stream so the PixieCrew could watch, too.

"Leah, just like this moment in my favorite ride, you have expanded my world beyond what I ever thought my life could be. You breathe magic and wonder into my being, challenging me in the best possible ways. Life with you is an adventure I want to live for a lifetime. You are the horizon I want to chase every day, my treasure that far surpasses any silver or gold."

I blushed. Lucas grinned.

"Princess Leah, my brilliant best friend, will you adventure with me like Marc and Alice? Like Walt and Lillian?"

Lucas paused to swallow, and I held my breath as fat tears rolled down my cheeks.

"LeahMetotheMagic, will you marry me, my love?"

My brain was in chaos as the cannon balls rained down around us, the compressed air making splashes here and there that tossed cold water on my skin. The familiar uneasiness of the doubt of my own self-worth crept toward me, but I straightened my shoulders and shoved it away.

I was worthy of Lucas now. And I had always been worthy of love—I just hadn't let myself believe it.

And so, with a sob, I began violently nodding my head up and down.

"Yes. Yes, Lucas. *YES!*"

I threw my arms around him and kissed him hard, knocking him back onto the floor of the boat. I landed on top of him. Shouts and cheers rose up around us, echoing in the show building as the lights on the phones moved back and forth in celebratory, arcing waves. We both laughed and kissed and laughed again, until Lucas gasped, "The RING!"

"Oh! Oh no!" I exclaimed as I sat up on the bench seat and desperately looked around. The boats around us grew quietly tense. "You didn't throw it overboard, did you??" I gripped the side of the boat and peered into the murky water, terrified that my exuberance might have sent the ring to Davy Jones' Locker.

"I found it!" Lucas held up the box triumphantly, and I breathed a huge sigh of relief.

To a second chorus of cheers and shouts of congratulations, Lucas took out the simple diamond ring and slipped it onto my left hand.

I grinned down at it like an idiot. It was perfect. Not a huge gaudy diamond but not tiny either, it suited me and fit like I had worn it for a lifetime. Lucas reached for me, his fingers sliding into the hair on either side of my face as his lips met mine once, then again, and then once more in a lingering kiss that sealed our promise to adventure together, wherever life might lead.

And then I knew it was time.

Pulling back, I looked into Lucas's blue eyes, needing him to see me, to fully receive the words I had held for so long.

"Lucas?"

"Yes, Leah my love?"

"I need to ask you something."

Lucas laughed, holding up my hand with the ring perched on my finger up to his mouth and kissing it gently.

"You have a lifetime to ask me any questions you want, love."

I swallowed.

This was it.

I reached down into the inner pocket of my park bag, carefully taking out the small velvet pouch I had kept safe just for this moment, knowing even months before that it was coming, eventually.

"Lucas, I see you. You are a giver. You give to your friends, you give to your followers, you give to your family, and you have given everything and more to me. I've watched you sacrifice and choose others over yourself, even stupidly coming after me when it almost got you killed."

I looked at him pointedly, and he just lifted an eyebrow at me, pairing it with a knowing smile. We'd had this fight many times before, and he always ended it by saying he had to rescue his Princess in order to have endless access to kissing me.

I blushed, reading his look, but I was determined not to let it distract me from my purpose.

"Never in my whole life have I met someone so dedicated to not only teaching people about why Disney is special but actually personally living out what Walt's dream was all about. You make magic in ways that some people will never fully understand or even appreciate. But I see you. I see your kind heart and your sharp wit. I see your late nights and your early mornings. I've seen you choose love when you could have given up. And I see you choose me, every day."

"So, my dear Lucas, my question is this. Will you choose me as your companion to venture forth with, into the unknown? Will you let me give all the love you show others back to you, every day for the rest of our lives?"

Studying his shining eyes before me, I pulled a small gold ring out of the pouch, engraved with symbols from all our favorite Disney attractions, and held it up to him.

"Will you, LucaDisNerd, choose to be my husband?"

In less than a heartbeat, Lucas slipped the ring on his finger and pulled me to him in a crushing embrace. While our entourage cheered and hollered around us, stomping their feet on the bottom of their bateaux, Lucas kissed me again and again before whispering fiercely in my ear, "I will be everything for you. Your husband. Your friend. Your biggest cheerleader. Your love. As you are mine, Leah, so I am, and will forever be, yours."

Epilogue

Colette

As I looked through the lens of my camera, I took what had to be the two-thousandth picture of my best friend and her new fiancé. The love and passion between them as they sat together in the back row of their bateau was unmistakable. The phone lighting wasn't the most flattering, but it was the best solution Lucas had for proposing in such a dark place.

I was glad our Cast Member friends had been so kind about us making this arrangement, not only to have commandeered three boats with our crew, but also to pause the ride in a specific place, just for a few moments, to allow Lucas and Leah to make a memory. They didn't have to do it, and we had felt bad asking, but when we revealed the "why" behind our ask, and when we shared all that Lucas and Leah had been through, the Disney Cast Members were all too happy to help bring a little extra pixie dust into the proposal.

I knew Leah had held onto that ring for Lucas for a while now, and I grinned as she returned his proposal in kind. But just as they embraced again for the second time, my camera drifted ever so slightly past Leah's shoulder, till my focus fell on someone I shouldn't be allowing in my view.

Eric.

He was perched on the seat in front of Leah and Lucas, diligently chatting with her live stream and laughing gaily at their candor. He was mesmerizing. And intoxicating.

And entirely off-limits.

But my finger didn't get the memo, because it ever-so-slightly pushed down on the shutter until I heard the sharp *click*, capturing his face, illuminated by the cellphone and lit up with joy for his friends.

It was then that his gaze snapped up. He looked directly at me, his smile dropping and his eyes growing intense. Like he knew.

Like he was remembering, too.

With a sharp intake of breath, I hurriedly hid behind the lens of my camera, snapping pics of the happy couple as they snuggled up together, and our boat began to slide forward in the water once more.

Eric turned back around, facing forward, and I breathed a sigh of relief.

But as we belted out X. Atencio's iconic pirate song together in a delightful chorus, I wondered how long this would go on with Eric and me, and where our ride would end.

Eric

The chat was flying. Congratulations, celebrations, and so many happy people were sending their love to Leah and Lucas via Leah's live stream, now well over 10,000 people as word had spread like wildfire about their proposal.

Back out under the starry Anaheim sky, our group made its way to Lucas's second surprise for Leah: A moonlight cruise on the *Mark Twain* after the park closed, with a live jazz band and free Mint Juleps and beignets for all.

Princess Tiana herself swept up between the two lovebirds, escorting them both onto the iconic steamship. Leah had tears streaming down her face the whole time.

As we sailed away from the dock, the band kicked it into high gear, and I diligently live streamed it all for Leah's online friends, knowing they didn't want to miss a thing, but also trying to free Leah up to simply enjoy her night without a phone in her hand while she danced with her new fiancé.

I zoomed in on Lucas and Leah for a quick minute, letting everyone online see a glimpse of the magic that was their relationship before pulling the camera back to shots of the band, the food, and the softly lit scenery floating by.

As I carried the phone over to the railing, melancholy swept over me. I was so happy for my friends, that they found each other and fit perfectly together. Not like some people.

Not like me and Colette.

I turned around and my eyes drifted without my permission, seeking her in the crowd. She was wearing a sparkly green dress accentuating every curve, and she danced more enthusiastically than Louis the Alligator from *The Princess and the Frog*. I laughed at her antics, mesmerized by her brazen pursuit of fun.

She had no idea the effect she had on me.

Ms. PixieDst: *Hey, why are we watching Colette dance?*

User7843298474: *I dunno, but the girl's got MOVES*

Ohana626: *She looks so free and happy*

MinnieMags: *Colette always looks so beautiful. You should ask her to dance, Eric*

Glancing down at the chat, I realize my habit of pointing the phone at whatever I focused on had backfired on me. I abruptly pulled Leah's phone away and refocused it back on the happy couple, laughing at the responses in the chat.

"Sorry Mags, my dance card is already full up as I've been tasked with entertaining you lovely ladies and gents while the lovebirds over there party like it's 1955. Besides, I wouldn't want to get *too* close to the action, lest I be swarmed by my dozens of admirers all at once."

The chat groaned and rolled their eyes at my antics, which was a perfect distraction away from the fact that there was, in all truth, only one woman I'd want to dance with on this floating vessel.

I flipped the camera around and thanked everyone for being part of the special night, explaining that it was now time I hand them back to Lucas and Leah for a final farewell.

Making my way to the newly-engaged couple currently swaying together on the dance floor to the classic Nat King Cole tune "Stardust," I tapped Leah on the shoulder and gestured to the phone. She pulled back from Lucas and took it from me, but not without first saying thank you and giving me a kiss on the cheek to express her gratitude.

I cleared my throat and waved her off, saying it was nothing. Because, really, I didn't do much. How hard was it to be friendly to a couple thousand super happy people on the most magical night ever for Lucas and Leah?

I made my way off the dance floor, determined to distance myself from thoughts of the gorgeous woman I had no business admiring when someone accidentally slammed into me with their Mint Julep in hand. I jumped back and spun around to avoid it sloshing all over the front of my vintage Pendleton plaid shirt.

Unfortunately, moving so suddenly also threw me off-balance, and before I knew what was happening, I fell into the group dancing behind me, landing awkwardly face-down on one of them.

Specifically, one in a green dress.

And she looked mad.

Lucas

My world felt complete with Leah wrapped up in my arms. A more perfect night had never existed, and I sighed in contentment as I whirled her around and around to the waltzing melody of "Ma Belle Evangeline." Gathering her closer, I sang the words to her as I had so many months ago in front of this very river we now floated upon as our dream came true before our eyes. Words about how she lit up my night, and how her heart belonged to me.

My voice caught on that phrase. Leah noticed, slowing our dance and pulling her hands to the sides of my face, as if needing to connect in a private moment amidst the throng of friends and family.

"Only you, Lucas. My heart belongs to only you. Forever."

Her eyes searched mine, wanting me to understand, needing my full attention.

She had it, always. I would never *not* be wholly focused on Leah. She held every part of my being within her graceful, intelligent soul.

"You are my Ray, Lucas."

Leah swallowed, emotion choking her words and making them shimmer upon delivery.

"And I will forever be your Evangeline. The second star to your right."

She buried her head in my shoulder, nuzzling into my neck. "Oh, how I love you, Lucas."

I couldn't hold back. Ducking my head, I captured her mouth with my own, demonstrating every emotion I couldn't adequately put into words by deepening our connection, meeting her mouth again and again, needing her to understand how I felt.

The band shifted their tune to play the haunting refrain of "Stardust," and I settled Leah in close to my chest, contentment sneaking over me like a warm blanket as I held the woman I loved in my arms.

But then Leah startled, pulling back and turning as she noticed Eric. He held her phone out to her, and she laughed. She thanked him, giving him a kiss on the cheek that made my breath catch with a quick stab of jealousy before checking myself. This was *Leah*. I didn't need to worry.

Eric waved a hand in goodbye, and Leah chatted with her online crew, showing them her ring and looking adorably, deliriously happy.

Which is why she didn't notice the chaos that had just happened behind her.

Out of the corner of my eye, I saw Eric fall and winced as he tumbled toward the floor. Then I recognized who he had fallen on, and my wincing turned into a full-body cringe.

This wasn't going to be good.

Leah felt me tense up.

"What's wrong?"

I nodded my chin in the direction of the current disaster, and Leah breathed out a simple, "Oh, *no*."

We looked on helplessly as Eric lay sprawled on top of Colette, her gorgeous emerald green dress torn halfway up her thigh. He quickly moved off of her but didn't distance himself. After a minute of leaning over her with what seemed like an intense conversation, he abruptly stood up, made his apologies, and offered a hand to Colette, which she pointedly refused. She stormed off, and Eric stalked away in the opposite direction.

I just shook my head.

"I don't know if those two will ever figure it out."

Leah sighed.

"Well, we'll be there for them if and when they need us. But tonight is our night, Lucas. I know you always want to help, but maybe they need some space to sort through everything on their own."

"Yeah, maybe. Plus I have the world's most beautiful woman in my arms right now, and I am not about to let her go."

Leah giggled, and I lowered my head to place soft kisses up the column of her neck, our audience be damned. A few catcalls reached our ears, but mostly everyone just clinked their mint julep glasses, demanding a proper kiss. We obliged, holding each other close as we steamed along on the Rivers of America in the moonlight, sailing toward our very own happily ever after.

A Note from the Author

The Imagineer John Hench (the one who lied about the Snow White fountain statue measurements) once rhapsodized about the meaning of Disneyland's Sleeping Beauty Castle, that it represents a stronghold, a place of safety. That was the inspiration for this book, the idea that Disneyland represents, for many of us, a place of safety and peace. While Leah found it to be a literal place of safety, more often we find that it's our hearts and souls that need respite at Disneyland more than our physical beings. How often do we gaze up at the castle and instantly feel at home? The worries of our everyday life become less, and our propensity for dreaming big dreams is amplified.

As a Disney content creator and live streamer myself (@disneycicerone, if you're curious), I did draw heavily on my own personal experience to create this work, but while my inspiration came from long days wandering around Disneyland, the characters here are from my own mind and are not meant to resemble any particular people in real life. I've enjoyed creating this fantasy Disneyland of the (somewhat near) future where I can let history take the forefront in a way that makes my historian heart happy.

Many thanks to my amazing early reader team who helped me refine and finesse this book into existence. Eliot, Jaque, Janis, Rhonda, Mary Helen, Kirk, Lindsey, and Kristin, thank you for your helpful feedback and support! An extra thanks to Kirk (@WalrusCarp) for being not only a creative sounding board, but also an encouraging friend who reminds me to lean into my imperfections and just keep swimming no matter what.

A very special thank you to my good friend, brilliant author, and expert editor Cidney Swanson, who has taught me so much and given me generous amounts of help/patience/cheerleading as I adventured my way through the process of bringing this novel to life. She's also supplied me with endless Disney-inspired treats to help with the post-Disney trip blues, and for that, I shall be forever grateful.

Leah's Pixie Crew and Lucas's Raven Clan were of course inspired by my favorite online Disney community, which we call the WalrusCarp Pocketfam (& my little part of the pocket, the Distorian's Lounge). Thank you to all my online friends who volunteered names through our Discord server for the members of these Pocketfam-esque communities. This book would not exist without Pocketfam's love and continued support, and I am so very grateful to have such wonderful Disney nerd friends in my life.

Finally, thank you to my family who has supported me throughout this process ... my three children who have (begrudgingly) accepted that mom now goes to Disney often for "work." Thank you to my mom, who has watched said kids for hours on end so that I could escape to my local Starbucks to write without people asking me for more screen time or how long to microwave soup. Thank you to my dad, who took me to Disneyland for its 40th anniversary to see the Lion King parade (whose floats are now in the Festival of the Lion King!) and who shares my love of Disney details. And, last but never least, thank you to my dear husband Eliot, who loves me like Lucas loves Leah.

About the Author

As the owner and creator of Disney Cicerone, Kate is passionate about helping others experience Disney in more meaningful and magical ways, allowing them to fully understand why their love of Disney has personal and social value. Her writing and creative work explore the sociological, psychological, emotional, historical, and unique ways Disney's history and culture influence our lives. When not wandering in the Disney parks looking at rocks and crates, you can find Kate researching, writing, and posting on social media about obscure Disney history with a dash of encouragement.

Also By Kate Grasso

Books

A Glimpse of the Magic: Finding Ourselves in the Disney Story

This curated collection of musings about Disney is infused with obscure history that will inspire you to see the parks you love in a new way, encouraging you to slow down, look closer, and see your own story reflected in every magical moment.

Curious about what happened between Eric & Colette?

Never fear, their story is up next! *Where the Fireflies Dance* is book one in a new series featuring Disney history live streamers. Follow me on Amazon & social media to be the first to read their wild romance!

Social

For daily obscure Disney History with a dash of encouragement, follow me @disneycicerone on TikTok, Instagram, Facebook, and YouTube!

Podcast

Exploring the history of the Disney Parks (with a dash of the ridiculous!), the Distory with Kate and Kirk Podcast is an adventure into the fascinatingly obscure details that have made the Disney parks what they are today.

Blog & Website

Want to read more?

Visit the Disney Cicerone blog at disneycicerone.com

Contact

Questions about Disney? I'd love to hear from you!

Contact me anytime at disneycicerone@gmail.com

Bibliography

Gennawey, Sam. The Disneyland Story: The Unofficial Guide to the Evolution of Walt Disney's Dream. Keen Communications, 2014.

Goldberg, Aaron H. Buying Disney's World: The Story of How Florida Swampland Became Walt Disney World. 1st ed. Philadelphia: Quaker Scribe, 2021.

Goldberg, Aaron H. The Disney Story: Chronicling the Man, the Mouse & the Parks. Quaker Scribe Publishing, 2016.

Korkis, Jim. Kungaloosh! The Mythic Jungles of Walt Disney World. Edited by Bob McLain. Theme Park Press, 2021.

Mongello, Lou. The Disney Interviews. Vol. 1: Second Star Media, 2020.

Neary, Kevin F., Susan Neary, and Vanessa Hunt. Maps of the Disney Parks: Charting 60 Years from California to Shanghai. 1st ed. Los Angeles: Disney Editions, 2016.

Nolte, Foxx. Boundless Realms: Deep Explorations Inside Disney's Haunted Mansion. Inklingwood Press, 2020.

Smothers, Marcy. Walt's Disneyland: A Walk in the Park with Walt Disney. 1st ed. Los Angeles: Disney Editions, 2021.

Snow, Richard. Disney's Land. New York: Scribner, 2019.

Surrell, Jason, Marty Sklar, and Tom Fitzgerald. The Haunted Mansion: Imagineering a Disney Classic. 3rd ed. Los Angeles: Disney Editions, 2015.

Surrell, Jason. Pirates of the Caribbean: From the Magic Kingdom to the Movies. 1st ed. New York: Disney Editions, 2005.

Thomas, Bob. Walt Disney: An American Original. New York, NY: Hyperion, 1994.

Made in the USA
Middletown, DE
30 April 2025

74975889R00091